S0-EDK-762

Murder on Indian Creek

A Bishop Bone Murder Mystery

By Robert G. Rogers

Copyright © 2020 Robert G. Rogers
All rights reserved.

Also by Robert G. Rogers

Bishop Bone Murder Mystery Series
A Tale of Two Sisters
Murder in the Pinebelt
A Killing in Oil
The Pinebelt Chicken War
Jennifer's Dream
La Jolla Shores Murders
Murder at the La Jolla Apogee
No Morning Dew
Brother James and the Second Coming
The Taco Wagons Murders
He's a Natural
The Legal Assassin
Death of the Weed Merchant

Non-Series Murder Mysteries & Suspense/Thrillers
The Christian Detective
That La Jolla Lawyer
Runt Wade
The End is Near

Contemporary Dramas
French Quarter Affair
Life and Times of Nobody Worth a Damn

Historical Women's Fiction – Jodie Mae

Youth/Teen Action and Adventure
Lost Indian Gold
Taylor's Wish
Swamp Ghost Mystery
Armageddon Ritual

Children's Picture Storybook – Fancy Fairy

Chapter 1

Bishop Bone was in the fruit orchard at the front of his cabin on Indian Creek in the southern part of Mississippi, between Jackson, the capital and the Gulf Coast. It was June, hot and humid without a cloud in the sky.

He was in his sixties and in good shape with some age wrinkles showing in his face. He stood a bit over six foot and had a rugged look about him which came in handy for his job when he was handling somebody's problem. In between jobs, there was always something to do outside, and he was glad to have the time to do it. It kept his waist relatively flat and his weight about where it should be for his size.

Half the time, when he was working outside as he was then, he wore an old floppy tennis hat to cover the spot that had begun to show in the back and to shade his face from the hot Mississippi summer sun.

He owned the old log cabin and twenty-two acres not far from downtown Lawton. It sat on timbered columns on a bluff overlooking Indian Creek, which divided the property into almost equal parts. The cabin's stilts were high enough to keep it out of the water when the creek flooded during its "one hundred year" flood. On the far side of the creek, beavers had built a dam across a small branch that emptied into the creek. The damn formed a little pond for their stick-mud mounds.

A waterfall up the creek marked one boundary of the

plot, a gravel road to a fish camp on the creek marked the other. The waterfall wasn't a big one. It was more like a bump in the road only it was a bump in the creek.

His hair was a light brown with some gray creeping in at the temples. His eyes were green. He let his hair lay where it fell after a shower unless he had a case that required being with people. When that was on his agenda, he combed it.

His face showed some age lines accented by a sag here and there. He didn't mind but he also tried not to spend too much time in front of a mirror. No need to be reminded, he told himself.

In the afternoons his close friend, Kathy, came out to relax with him on the back porch of the cabin with something cold to drink while they watched the beavers work. Occasionally, canoeists floating past offered a diversion. They had to pull their canoes out of the creek and drag them around the falls going up stream. The braver of them, coming down stream, went over the falls on the side of the waterfall where there were no rocks. That side was relatively safe for those with experience to jet over.

A porch screen kept the mosquitoes and bugs outside. Bishop and Kathy especially enjoyed that asset when having their happy hour on the porch in the afternoons. The bugs including the mosquitoes spent their time bouncing off the screen, trying to get in for a bite of something human.

Kathy's face was more round than narrow, but pretty, and it didn't come with an ego, for which he was grateful. Shoulder length hair snuggled the contours of her face. She was a brunette but the beginnings of gray lightened it a shade. Her eyes were a golden brown. She was some years younger than Bishop but it had not been a problem. In addition to just enjoying each other's company, they also played tennis at one of the local courts and sometimes on the Country Club courts with friends who were Club members.

When she came up the stairs for a visit, which was almost every day, he pulled her close for a Mississippi hug and kiss and enjoyed the intoxicating fragrance that only a woman has, and hers, he figured, was the best. She wore a perfume called Shalimar, which he loved.

A Mississippi hug, as those around town knew, was one of those where the man and woman pulled each other body to body close.

Kathy managed the Lawton library and since they'd met he got all his reading material from it. Lawton, a small Mississippi town of under twenty-five thousand, an hour or so's drive north of the coast, was the county seat. Bishop's cabin was a few minutes south of the town.

Kathy always seemed so damned happy and her smile gave him a lift on the worst of days. He never passed up an opportunity to see her and always felt much better afterwards.

He still fought a depression that caught up with him now and then. It stemmed back to when he was more or less chased out of Los Angeles on a bogus fraud charge and ended up in Lawton. Fighting the charge had cost him his family and his professional status in California. He was an attorney and was able to later reverse the charge. He collected a good judgment in the process. Unfortunately, however, he could not reverse the damage to his family or to his professional status. So he stayed in Lawton and found Kathy.

A fortuitous stroke of luck the first night he was in town made him some lasting friends, and those friends introduced him to bankers who needed his expertise in connection with loans, which were in default. So, after becoming qualified as a Mississippi attorney, he helped banks "work out" their problem loans. He didn't need an office for that, just the phone he kept in his pocket.

*****

That afternoon, he was working in his fruit orchard along the driveway. It was separated from the road along the front of his property by woods so dense that he couldn't see vehicles traveling on it. He enjoyed the privacy.

He'd finished pruning the wild limbs that popped out of the canopies of the fruit trees from time to time. After he'd put the last limb on the pile he'd been accumulating, he heard a late model vehicle coming down the driveway. It stopped when the driver saw him in the orchard. It was a brown Ford truck, Bishop decided in a glance, as men generally do when they see a vehicle. It looked fairly new.

He had turned when he heard the truck and watched

4

as the occupants, a man and woman, got out. He wiped sweat off his forehead and took a cautious step in their direction.

Don't know 'em, he thought. The man was on the tall side and rough looking. He wore dungarees that showed some wear. *Work clothes,* Bishop thought.

Guy has to be half a foot over six feet. Must weigh close to two hundred. Big son of a bitch. Tough looking to boot. Grim face. Mean looking actually, if I wanted to be closer to reality. Women probably consider him ruggedly handsome. Likely in his late fifties or early sixties. Hasn't shaved in a day or so. Hope he didn't come to fight. He laughed to himself with an added thought. *If he did, maybe he's a slow runner.*

He glanced at the woman standing beside the man. She was also on the tall side, but skinny and really kind of plain looking. She wore no make-up. Her light hair hung down to her shoulders, probably brown Bishop figured from a quick look. *Needed combing,* he decided. No smile was on her face and it didn't look like any had ever troubled it for a visit.

She wore worn jogging togs and tennis shoes. *Younger than the guy. Late forties most likely. I wonder how they got together. She doesn't look like his type ... unless he knows she's not likely to mess around, like I'm betting he does. He probably has many temptations, and probably doesn't resist any a man would look twice at.*

They approached Bishop who was glad he had his heavy-duty pruning shears in his hands. He didn't know why they were there, and the unknown always made him suspicious.

When they were close, the man stuck out his hand and showed a slight smile. Forced, Bishop figured. *Can't be a salesman, with a smile like that.*

"Fletcher Watson," he said and with a nod at the woman, added, "My wife, "Julia.""

Voice sounds like it's being dragged over old gravel, Bishop thought as he shook the man's hand and let it go. It felt rough, and the man added a big squeeze to the shake. He had a bit of an accent, like he might have been born in the South or at least lived below the Mason-Dixon line for some time before moving away.

She offered a half-smile at Bishop, but for the most part maintained her stoic demeanor while they were there. She had good teeth, both did, Bishop noticed. He was relieved that they were smiling.

They didn't come to fight, he thought with a laugh that he kept to himself. He hadn't seriously thought they had, but always prepared himself for the worst case.

"Hello," she said and offered her hand for an introductory shake. She had a voice that belied her plain looking demeanor. It carried a confident tone like she might have been in charge of something at one time. She also had something of a southern accent.

Bishop nodded at both and gave his name. "Been working," he said with a wave at his orchard. The pear tree nearest him had plenty of pears. Two trees over, a peach tree looked like it was ready for harvesting. Likewise the fig tree next to it. It was full of ripe figs ready for plucking. He and Kathy were planning to do just that on the coming weekend. She knew a lady who would make fig jam for them for half the figs.

They planned to eat the pears and the other fruit as it ripened. Kathy had told him it was healthier that way … eating them off the trees.

"Looks good. All the trees. I hope we can do as well," Fletcher said. "We're buying the land down the road from you. We'll build. Plant when we can."

"The ground is good," Bishop said. "Creek overflowed this area in the past and left good top soil behind."

Watson nodded. As did Julia who looked north in the direction of their land.

Bishop knew the property. The acres along the road, probably ten or so acres, had been used for corn and soybeans since Bishop had been in residence. The rest of it, all the way to the creek, was heavily wooded.

"I had heard it was for sale," he said. "Decent sized piece." It comprised almost thirty-five acres with one side bordering the creek. The property line between that land and his was the creek's waterfall.

He'd heard the owner had been asking a hundred and fifty thousand dollars for it. Bishop imagined the price included some room for negotiation.

"We're going to clear a site down at the creek and build so we can sit out back and watch it run," Julia said with a nod in the direction of his cabin. "I imagine you do that."

Bishop agreed and said, "I haven't walked the piece but I imagine you'll have plenty of places to pick for a home with a view of the water. Boats come up and down the creek when it's warm. People having fun. We get a kick out of watching them."

"Some friends of ours heard we were interested in the area,'" Julia said. "They told us Bishop Bone lived out here. That's why we stopped by to say hello and to get your opinion. They spoke well of you. Said you helped the chief of Police now and then with his cases."

"You could probably run for office," Fletcher said without any feeling in his suggestion. He added one of those "don't give a damn" shrugs, Bishop decided.

"No," Bishop said. "I don't like kissing the hindmost of anybody, especially somebody whose vote I need. That's one reason I moved out here. To have privacy."

"I don't blame you," Julia said.

"D'you build?" Fletcher asked, pointing at Bishop's stilted cabin. Although some distance off the road, it was visible down the curved driveway, surrounded by ancient trees, pines and oaks mainly.

Bishop shook his head. "No. It was here. Hadn't been lived in for a while. I had to remodel … extensively. Added bathrooms. Redid the kitchen. Expanded some rooms. Put screens on the porches. Mosquitoes can get bad out here. Have to put on repellant when we go outside."

"You married," Julia asked.

Bishop realized he'd just said "we." He smiled. "No, Kathy and I are engaged. Been waiting for the right time to do it."

That wasn't the case, but he didn't want to go into

the details of their decision to just enjoy the comforts of each other's companionship without the necessity of a paper binding them to it.

"We're about the same," she said without elaboration. "Kind of married."

Bishop thought the man glanced at her and frowned slightly at her disclosure. So he elected discretion and didn't ask her anything about their relationship.

"Would you want to look my place over? May pick up some ideas," Bishop said, figuring that was why they'd dropped by.

Fletcher nodded and said, "If you wouldn't mind. We have a house in town now. We'll sell it when we get one built out here."

Bishop nodded his head to show his understanding.

He looked at Bishop and asked, "If you don't mind me asking, you don't seem to have a Southern accent. Where are you from?"

Bishop gave a half laugh. He wasn't about to tell him how he came to live there. He told him he'd had business in the state and while here, grew to like the people he'd met and the culture.

"So when I retired I moved here from California. Never regretted it." The crooked developer and corrupt banker who'd conspired to defraud him flashed through his mind, but he let it go. No way was he going to tell just anybody that story. Kathy knew, and one or two others, close friends. It had cost him his family and his legal practice but he'd recovered for the most part since he'd met Kathy. She was the love the fraud had taken from him.

"We were born in the Atlanta area. I was born in Atlanta. Julia just south of there. But we both worked in DC where we met," the man said. "We were in … property management but decided to … well, retire. We'd heard about Lawton and looked for land here. Found it and now we want to build."

"Good choice," Bishop said. They didn't look old enough to retire, but he didn't say anything. *Maybe they sold their business. Got enough to retire.*

Bishop turned and headed for the cabin at the end of his driveway.

"Wait," Fletcher said. "Hop in. We'll drive."

Julia opened the back door of the truck and Bishop climbed in. He lay his pruner on the floor.

*****

At the house, Bishop took them upstairs on what he called his "freight lift." It was supposed to have been an elevator, but while he was in San Diego for a speech and couldn't be reached, his contractor opted to install a lift that didn't cost as much. It made noise and was slow, but it got them up and down.

Bishop had stayed in California after the speech to help the chief of Police in San Diego on a case and missed the contractor's call. When asked about it later, the contractor explained that it was the best he could do at the time, so Bishop was living with it. He sure as hell wasn't going to pay to replace it.

Fletcher and Julia didn't complain about the noise. *Probably figured it was better than having to trudge up the steps,* Bishop thought.

Inside, he showed them around. They were impressed by the beams he and Kathy had installed on the ceilings. They were fake, but from the floor, they looked real. The kitchen was almost all new. That was Bishop's gift to Kathy. She liked to cook and needed the implements to be modern.

When they were done, Bishop offered them something to drink on the porch. Kathy wouldn't be there for a couple more hours. Bishop would enjoy another drink with her and tell her about the Watson's visit.

Fletcher and Julia had wine. Bishop took a beer. He also put out dishes of nuts for them all to munch on while they relaxed.

They sat in the porch chairs to stare at the creek and the beaver pond on the far side. As usual, the furred creatures were busy working.

Julia said she hoped they would have beavers along the creek where they were going to build.

"Maybe," Bishop said. "I was lucky the pond was there for them." He gestured across the creek. "Kind of a natural place for them to form a colony or whatever it is beavers have."

Fletcher nodded and said, "Colony is right, I believe,"

Bishop nodded.

"They're so industrious," Julia said.

11

"They work like robots," Bishop said. He looked at the man and asked, "You plan to start a new management company here?"

He didn't see how, considering the lack of much to manage in Lawton. There were apartment complexes around town and nearby as well as some condos, but mostly the local developers who'd built them did the management for a fee.

He figured they most likely knew that as well, but he asked to see if he could get more information out of them. He was curious about what they had been doing and why they had sold their business.

Fletcher looked at Bishop for a moment before saying, "No, we're going to kick back and enjoy being retired. I may write a book or two. Julia likes to paint. I imagine she'll have a studio. Nothing serious, in the way of work, for either of us."

So, he's not going to elaborate, Bishop thought. *Okay.*

"Well, with a property as big as yours is, you'll certainly stay busy just taking care of it. When I'm not on a case for a client, I'm taking care of one thing or another around here," Bishop said. "Keeps me busy."

He briefly explained how he handled bank problems. Loans that were in default that the banks labeled "workouts." When given an assignment, he'd meet with the borrowers to see if the loan could be saved. Usually he found a solution to save it and the business it encumbered. If not, he'd recommend foreclosure or negotiate to have the borrower sell the property and give the proceeds from the sale to the bank. In those cases, the banks didn't lose money even though the borrowers usually did. However, they lost less with a sale than they would have on a straight foreclosure.

"Sounds like work," Fletcher said of Bishop's work. "I don't think we'd want that much aggravation."

"That's right, Bishop," Julia added. "We settled up in DC to get rid of all the pressure that comes from working with people. We're going to take it easy down here. Travel some. I'll paint, like Fletcher said. Might do a little church work. Already am, in fact. We joined the First Methodist Church in Lawton when we moved here."

"We've been in town for about three years now," Fletcher explained. "Been looking for a place to buy out of town. Finally decided to buy some land and build on it. We wanted a water view, like yours." He pointed to the creek. Its waters were running green just then. It hadn't rained in a few weeks. When it rained, the water turned light brown from the clay in the area.

A layer of clay ran through that part of Mississippi, which was known as the Pine Belt, since pine trees thrived in it. For years, the lumber industry also thrived in the Pine Belt, milling out lumber from the harvested pines. Then oil was discovered and lumber had to share the land with the well drillers.

"Good idea," Bishop said. "Building a house can be a lot of fun, even remodeling like we did. It's a creative undertaking."

"That's what we think too," Julia said. "We're

looking forward to it. We have an architect. As soon as the escrow closes, we'll get him started."

"Give me your phone number so Kathy and I can invite you to dinner."

Fletcher took out a pen and wrote down their phone number and address in Lawton. He handed the paper he'd written it on to Bishop who stuck it in his shirt pocket.

"I added my email. Sometimes easier to send an email these days than calling," he said.

"I agree. Thanks," Bishop said as he glanced at it. "I prefer emails."

They finished their wine and left.

*****

Kathy arrived later with barbequed chicken for their dinner. Bishop told her about the visit from Fletcher and Julia.

"I'm not sure about their relationship, but his last name is Watson. Maybe hers is too. I'm just not sure." He told her why, her comment about being 'kind of married.'

Kathy also thought it sounded odd but didn't have any more of an explanation than Bishop had.

"So, we're going to have neighbors," she said as they enjoyed their happy hour on the back porch. Bishop had mixed G and Ts for them. He gave her a summary of their visit including their plans.

"When are they going to build?" she asked.

Bishop wasn't sure, but figured within the next sixty days or so. They had to finish their plans and get a building permit.

"I don't know if they have a contractor. May put the job out for bids," he said. "Takes a while to get through all that. Plus, they have to cut a driveway through the trees to get back to where they want to build. I don't imagine they'll have to build on stilts. From what they said, where they want to put the house is on a bit of a hill. The architect and engineer figure three feet off the ground will be okay."

"That'll save some time and money," she said.

Bishop told her that they'd apparently sold their management company in DC and had enough money so neither had to work. They hadn't said that for sure, but that was his understanding from what was said.

"Must have done all right," she said.

Bishop agreed.

Chapter 2

Clyde Jenkins, the chief of the Lawton police department, came out at noon the next day with more of the story about Bishop's new neighbors. They had coffee. Bishop had one of those machines that ground the coffee beans so every cup was fresh.

They'd become good friends after Bishop had helped him with a number of police cases over the years. He and his wife, June, were frequent dinner guests.

Bishop told him about the visit of Fletcher and Julia the day before.

"Be damned," Jenkins said. "Came by, did they? I know about the Watsons, a little anyway. Haven't met 'em yet. Might one day though."

That sounded suspicious to Bishop prompting a quest for more information.

"The guy's going to be my neighbor," Bishop told the chief. "Tell me what you've heard. Should I keep my shotgun handy? He told me they were in property management in DC. Probably sold the business but they didn't say for sure. I just got that impression."

Julia had said they'd settled up and he'd said they'd retired. Nothing definite about selling the business.

"Yeah. That's the story I got as well. I think they did sell the business. From what I hear, the women around town think he's … well, a real man." The chief laughed and flexed his muscles. "When they talk to him, they stand as close as they dare and hug him or put their hands on him at the least provocation."

"I can understand that. Hell, he could be a movie star. You know playing one of those tough guys staring down bad guys with beautiful women on each arm."

"Right. Just rumors you understand, but I've heard that he's taken advantage of their interest."

"I don't imagine that goes over much with their husbands," Bishop said.

Jenkins nodded. "He hasn't been caught at it, if you know what I mean. Just talk, but where there's smoke there's fire."

"I agree. Hell, even city guys own shotguns. If the talk sounds like one of their wives is involved, old Fletcher might want to watch his back."

"Yeah. For sure nobody's gonna go face to face with him. Tough looking son of a gun like that," Jenkins said.

Bishop agreed.

"He is married though. That ought to slow him down some."

"Got a curve in that road, Chief. Julie, the woman who was with him, said they were only 'kind of married' – like me and Kathy."

As he said that, he thought, *I wonder if she meant they were married but he still fooled around. That could be a kind of marriage, I suppose.*

Bishop's relationship with Kathy was a private thing. The chief knew, but following polite protocol never brought it up.

The chief frowned. "Wonder what the hell she meant by that? Either you're married or you're not. I thought he was married. I think that's what people around town think."

"I got the impression that they just have a relationship, like me and Kathy. Not that I give a damn." He told him what he'd just thought Julia might have been alluding to, considering the rumors circulating about the man.

"Son of a gun," Jenkins said. "If that gets out, I'd say he should watch his back. But that might not be a problem when he moves out here."

"Unless he keeps going to church in town. No Methodist churches around here. Probably lots of women go to church with active hormones," Bishop said with a grin. "Humans haven't evolved past their hormones. Procreation is always on our tables."

The Creator made the process enjoyable and that favored procreation. Unfortunately, it also caused some problems that the churches and the laws have tried to solve with only partial success, he thought.

"So true, Bishop. Well, not my problem anyway. Not yet," Jenkins replied. "And I hope it never shows up in my office. It'll be the sheriff's problem if anything happens out here." The sheriff's name was Jim Thompson. His friends called him Jim, sometimes Big Jim. He stood several inches over six feet and had the look of a lawman who could go head to head with a bad guy if necessary.

"I get you," Bishop said. The sheriff usually had jurisdiction over crimes that were perpetrated in the country. However, he and the chief often worked together on cases.

Chief Jenkins finished his coffee, told Bishop goodbye and headed back to his office. "See you for beer when I'm next out this way," he said as he left.

"There's always a bottle or two in the fridge," Bishop said with a laugh.

*****

Soon afterward Bishop began seeing trucks and other equipment headed onto the Watson's property. It appeared they were cutting a driveway through the woods to a site for the house the Watson's wanted to build. When the number of trucks and equipment coming and going began to diminish, Bishop figured the driveway was almost completed, so he drove down the dirt lane to check out their progress.

Fletcher was standing there with what appeared to be the supervisor of the crew working on the road, a heavy-set man in a short-sleeved shirt and work pants. The man appeared to be uncomfortable.

Probably for a good reason. Fletcher looks like he is running the show, telling the man's crew what to cut and what to do afterwards, Bishop thought. *I'd guess the supervisor doesn't like it much.*

Some of men were cutting the last of trees on the site, big and small, and loading the timber onto trucks to be hauled away. *Sold to a lumber company,* Bishop supposed.

Others, responding to Fletcher's direction, were

grinding the larger stumps into nothing and loading the sawdust onto the trucks. Now and then, Fletcher would direct that some of the debris, mostly the sawdust, be put into holes here and there.

Bishop got out of his jeep and walked over to where they stood. He could see the river through the trees and bushes on the slope in front of where they stood.

The two men turned when they saw him drive up but barely acknowledged it. When Bishop got close, Fletcher shoved out his hand with a thin smile to shake Bishop's. The supervisor noted Bishop's presence with a hello and reluctant smile.

"Hard at it," Bishop said.

Fletcher agreed. "Want to start building as soon as we can. Have to clear the damn site first. People work like they got lead in their asses." He waved at the men working the equipment on the site.

The supervisor looked at him with a frown but said nothing. The man with the check book was the "boss" but Bishop knew from his experiences with people that the supervisor probably didn't like it a bit. It was his job to direct his men; to let somebody else do it usually led to disrespect.

I bet his poor wife has to listen to his bitching at night when he's drinking his nightly beer.

"When are you figuring on starting to build?" Bishop asked.

Fletcher moved away and motioned for Bishop to follow him. Bishop assumed he wanted to talk away from the supervisor and the others working on clearing the trees from the site.

Responding to Bishop's question, he said, "I'd guess in a couple of weeks. Our plans are for a farmhouse look, a rustic cabin with wood siding, a shingled roof. We have a contractor already. I need to clear some more of the lower bushes off the slope, maybe prune more of the tree limbs … open up the view, and clear enough for a decent fire break. This bunch can do some of that while the building is going on."

"Sounds like a good plan," Bishop said.

"I think so. I was coming over to see you today. You have contacts in town, I understand. The work you've done for the police stands you in good stead. People speak highly of you."

"I don't know about that, but thank you." Bishop figured something was coming. People like Fletcher Watson don't throw out compliments for nothing. And he was right.

"The dumb ass permit people want me to install a tin roof instead of the wood shakes my architect proposes and Julia and I want."

"Fire protections, most likely," Bishop said.

"That's what they say, but I think they're full of shit." He waved his arm about. "Hell, that's why I'm cutting all the trees to make sure I don't have anything that'll burn close to the house. I'm asking you as my neighbor to talk to the permit people, maybe the supervisors, and tell them you have a shake roof and you haven't had a fire problem," Fletcher said.

"My cabin was built before tin roofs were available.

I didn't have to get a building permit to remodel," Bishop said.

Fletcher ignored that and said, "If you'll put in a word for me, your bank account will look a lot better, if you know what I mean. Give me a number."

As Bishop opened his mouth to reply, Fletcher pulled out his wallet, glanced to see if anybody was watching, and shoved six one hundred dollar bills at him.

"Pass these around. Money gets these yokels attention. That's all I have right now, but I'll get more and make it worth your while if I get my permit without the tin roof requirement."

Bishop was surprised and said, "I thank you for your comments, Fletcher. And, I appreciate your concerns and preferences, but –"

Fletcher interrupted and said, "But you won't do it, is that what you're going to say? You won't help a neighbor. You could do it in a word but you're too damn scared. Is that it? What a wimp! Get the hell out of my sight."

"You can kiss my ass," Bishop said. "You asked me to bribe public officials. I won't do it. Hell, I should report you but I'll let it go. But don't call me another name or we'll be on the ground and we won't be talking! Understand me? Good luck. With your arrogant, I could add stupid, attitude, you're gonna need it."

Bishop stormed away before he could answer. The workers watching Bishop leave figured the men had had a disagreement. They smiled their approval.

Not only is he a mean son of a bitch, he's arrogant and thinks his way is the only way. I bet his smile is afraid to be on his face for very long. No wonder the tree clearing supervisor keeps his mouth shut.

He gave Kathy a report that evening. "Fletcher wants to start building in a couple of weeks."

He told her Fletcher's problem about getting the permit. How he'd rejected the man's request that he intervene on his behalf and spread money around.

"What?" She said. "I can't believe anybody would do that. That's … well, isn't it bribery?"

"I think so. And told him as much. He wasn't a happy camper." Bishop told her about their exchange.

"I doubt it would have taken much more from me before he would have started swinging," he said.

"I'm glad you walked away," she told him.

"Me too."

"I imagine they'll have to build up the drive way some. Has some low spots that'll need dirt and culverts under it to keep water from backing up. Otherwise the drive way will be a dam for a pond."

In ancient times, the creek or a tributary had a branch that crossed the land. The driveway had to cross through it to reach the site for the house overlooking the creek.

*****

Later Kathy had heard that Fletcher had his building permit and had begun construction. And he would have a wood shingled roof.

People gossiped when they came into the library and she overheard some of it. And, sometimes they took the time to tell her. New people in town generated gossip about what they were doing, and especially the Watsons with what Fletcher had been doing creating the news.

When she told Bishop, he said, "Well, I guess he got somebody else to spread a little money around."

"Glad it wasn't you," she said.

"No way," he said.

*****

After building had begun, Bishop drove by the Watson's building site a few times to "rubber neck" the progress. That's what he called it. He did it from a distance, on the driveway, to avoid having another confrontation with Fletcher.

They brought in stones, instead of bricks, for the foundation to raise the house off the ground. It was about four feet high. Then they unloaded the beams and lumber and began building. As he had done with the crew clearing the site, Fletcher shouted orders at the crew doing the building. Bishop could hear him from where he'd stopped.

The supervisor of that crew didn't appear to like it any more than the supervisor of the tree clearing crew, Bishop observed and when Fletcher got too involved supervising his crew, he would grab Fletcher's arm and tell him something. Bishop assumed he was telling him to back off.

Most crews preferred having only one boss. Fletcher, even with his checkbook, couldn't overcome that culture.

A month after they'd begun building, Chief Jenkins came out for an afternoon beer.

"Got some interesting news about your neighbor," he told Bishop as he took his bottle and sat down. "Just came from over there. Curiosity got the better of me and I was already out that way on another call I had to make. I got there just in time to see the end of a pretty good fight."

"Well hell, tell me. I hope it was a juicy one."

"Pretty close to a knock down and drag out." The chief then told Bishop what had happened.

"From what I was told, Fletcher was making an ass of himself, bossing the building crew. The crew's supervisor told Fletcher to tell him what he wanted done. If he agreed, he'd tell his crew to do it.

"We're building your house according to the plans and specs so back off. It confuses the hell out of the crew to have two bosses," the supervisor told him.

Fletcher nodded his head like he was agreeing, but that was all. He ignored the man and kept issuing orders to the building crew. Then one day the owner of the construction company came out and threatened to pull off the job if Fletcher didn't stop interfering. And he'd have his attorney sue Fletcher for breach of contract."

"Damn. Sounds like Fletcher was shooting himself in the foot."

Jenkins laughed, "He sure as hell was. Well, he kind of agreed with the owner but as soon as the man drove away, Fletcher jumped right back in and started bossing the building crew like he had been doing."

"Son of a bitch!"

"Right. Son of a bitch. The regular crew chief objected and shoved Fletcher. You know Fletcher's no weakling. Tough assed son of a bitch if you want to call a spade a spade."

"I'd say. Big bastard," Bishop added.

"Well, they went at it and some of the crew joined in. Old Fletcher was holding his own though, giving about as much as he was taking. Even so, blood was flowing: both Fletcher's and the others. His wife, Julia, was out there and she called the sheriff when they started fighting. The sheriff and some deputies came out to stop it before anybody was killed. He told me from the look of it, Fletcher might have been the one on the ground when it was over."

"The sheriff arrest anybody?"

"Well, he asked what had happened. Like I told you. Looked like the crew might have started it but it wasn't all that clear. Thing is, nobody wanted to press charges. So the sheriff wrote it up and left. Fletcher's wife patched him up. The building crew did the same for their guys," Jenkins said.

"What about the job? Did they pull off the job?" Bishop asked.

"By the time they'd stopped the bleeding, the owner had shown up. He was there when I was. He and Fletcher had a face to face. From what I could hear, Fletcher agreed to let the crew build. He'd watch and if he had anything to say, he'd tell the crew chief. If that didn't work, he'd tell the owner. But he would not give the crew any orders. When I left, they were going back to work like nothing had happened."

"Be damned, that is some pretty juicy news. I can see it in my mind. Fletcher surrounded by the building crew swinging two by fours," Bishop said with a laugh.

"That's about it. But I can tell you this, Fletcher was knocking some ass and Julia was helping him do it. She grabbed up a two by four and was knocking heads."

"That would have been worth seeing," Bishop said.

"I wish I had showed up in time to see it myself. Had to get it second hand," Chief Jenkins said, turning up his bottle. "Could use another. I'll get it."

Bishop shook his head and got up to get him a refill.

He said, "I guess they had to have a showdown. Fletcher is apparently used to having his way. And, big as he is, I guess most people don't argue."

"I guess. But this time there were enough crew members to convince him that a little discretion might be the better part of valor," Jenkins said with a smile.

Bishop brought him a refill. They usually only had one bottle each, but in the excitement of telling the story, the chief drank faster.

Bishop related the confrontation he'd had earlier with Fletcher about the tin roof requirement and how that almost ended in a brawl.

"He's an arrogant son of a bitch," Bishop said. "I'm glad we didn't come to blows."

"Me too. I might have been buying my beer in town.

He must have somehow convinced the folks issuing the permit to back off," the chief said.

"I won't guess about how he convinced them," Bishop said.

"Me either, and since I have no proof of any wrong doings, I'm not going to make waves," the chief added.

Bishop agreed.

Kathy came up the stairs a few minutes later. Bishop gave her a summary of the story. She said she wasn't surprised. She'd heard some women say that some husbands around town might also be gearing up to have a confrontation with Fletcher.

*****

That came a couple of weeks later. One evening, after dark, somebody fired a shotgun blast through the Watson's living room window. Nobody was hurt and there were no witnesses. The chief chalked it up to a husband who was sending Fletcher a message.

He called Bishop with the story. "Somebody left a note in their mail box. It said if he didn't 'keep it zipped up' the next shot would relieve him of having to."

Bishop laughed. "Some guy with too little in the way of muscles or guts or maybe just too damn smart to take Fletcher on face to face, resorted to a little discretion. Any idea who did the shooting?"

"No. Hell, it could have been any number of men. I've heard old Fletcher is generous with his philandering. Aims to please."

"I wonder how Julia puts up with it?" Bishop asked.

"It's not like she has many options. She's not exactly a beauty queen," Chief Jenkins said.

Bishop agreed. His first impression was that she was pretty plain.

"I wonder how they got together in the first place?" Bishop said. "They worked together. She must have had something on him. Or hell, maybe he wanted somebody who had to take it. It's not like she'd be in great demand."

"If I were in her shoes, I'd get a divorce and take the son of a bitch for all she could get."

"Who knows?" Bishop said. "They may have a prenuptial agreement."

"If you say so. You'd know," the chief said. He promised to come out that weekend and do a little fishing.

"I may let you do it by yourself. I've got some yard work to do. I've been putting it off. But we can have a beer after you've caught all my fish," Bishop said.

"Deal."

*****

The confrontation Fletcher had with the building crew must have worked. Bishop didn't hear of any other fights, and the building of the house went smoothly from what he could see when he drove over. Julia was always there walking around outside. If she saw him in the driveway, rubbernecking, she gave no indication.

Maybe she reminds Fletcher that he can look but not boss. She makes sure peace prevails and Fletcher seems calm. Stays out of the way. House looks good. Rustic farmhouse. Looks like it's a hundred years old. Wood siding. Architect did a good job, Bishop thought.

When Julia and Fletcher were distracted, and with carpenters all over, Bishop took the time to walk through the house. The interior looked good too, very livable. He was on site when the furniture was unloaded but didn't go in. Julia and Fletcher were part of that, making sure that each piece went where they wanted it to go.

And when it was all done, the neighbors, such as they were, half a dozen along the road including Bishop and Kathy, were invited to a house warming. Nobody turned down the invitation. The Watsons were news. Bishop lived the closest to them.

Julia must have prevailed on him to invite us, Bishop thought. *Or he just plain forgot what an ass he'd made of himself trying to get me to offer bribes so he could get a wooden roof.*

Fletcher and Julia divided their time greeting the guests. Bishop and Kathy ended up with Fletcher.

When he saw Bishop, his lips turned up in a snarl and he said, "I guess you can see I have wooden shingles on my roof. No fuckin' tin. Not all the people in this town are gutless."

He turned and walked away before Bishop could answer, but it offended him. But not as much as he would he would be offended later.

They barbequed steaks in the back yard overlooking the creek. Guests helped, and watched until their steaks were cooked the way they wanted them. Wine, beer, and harder stuff was available to drink. Music played from a player set up near the BBQ, competing with the singing of birds all around.

The thing that pissed Bishop off was the attention Fletcher was paying Kathy when she and Bishop were separated. Once, after he'd given Kathy a big squeeze, Bishop hurried over and took his arm from around her waist. He looked the man in the face and said, "Fletcher, I don't know what you do with the other women in Lawton, and don't care. It's none of my business. But Kathy *is* my business, and I get pissed in a hurry when anybody messes with her. Your definition of gutless 'll have to be adjusted. Understand!"

Bishop didn't know how he'd handle the guy if Fletcher wanted to fight about it, but he thought of a couple of things he could do to stay alive. *Rush the bastard and give him a head butt under his chin. And, while he was chewing on that, use my knee to render his pissing part out of order. And if that doesn't work, I guess Kathy will be visiting me in the hospital.*

Fletcher shoved out a right hand to poke Bishop in the shoulder with his finger but Bishop knocked it away with his arm and got ready. He waited half a second and watched for Fletcher's next move. He figured Fletcher was tensing up to start swinging, but Julia, who was a step away, called out, "Fletcher! They are our neighbors for God's sake!"

Fletcher blinked and stared at her for a couple of seconds before his fists relaxed. He looked at Bishop standing in front of him and said, "Sorry. I got carried away. Sorry." He turned and left.

Bishop let out a breath of air. He didn't know if he could have stopped the guy with a head butt, but was glad he didn't have to try.

Kathy gave him a big hug. "You're my hero, Bishop. I was about to tell him to back off. I'm glad you did it for me. It meant more for you to do it, I'm sure of that."

"Julia was smart," Bishop said. "That bastard uses his size to push people around. Gonna catch up with him one of these days."

"I hope you're not the one having to do it," Kathy said. "But if you are, he'll find out you can push with the best of them."

He thanked her. *I wonder. I'm glad I didn't have to find out today.*

They left early. Bishop told her on the way home that they would be out of town the next time they were invited over.

Kathy laughed. "I agree."

*****

A few weeks later, Bishop was outside working in the garden he'd planted for Kathy. It was noon but Bishop didn't pay any attention to the time. He was only concerned with the job.

Kathy wanted fresh vegetables and he obliged her by

clearing an area and planting what she said she wanted. He thought he'd heard a gunshot followed by another one coming from the Watson's property. At that distance they weren't too loud, but he could hear them.

Wondering what he's shooting at? Deer and other creatures roamed the area. He'd seen them on his land, but so far, they hadn't been enough of a nuisance for him to worry about.

"Fletcher has a short fuse, I guess," Bishop said. "Shoots anything that's moving."

An hour or so later, Chief Jenkin's car pulled down the drive. Bishop was winding up his work for the day. He walked over to greet his friend. It had been a couple of weeks since a bank had any jobs for him, so he'd been working on things around their cabin.

"Bishop," Jenkins said. "I was just over at the Watson's. Somebody killed the bastard, Fletcher. Yep, shot him with a shotgun. Probably a 410 gauge but they won't know for sure until they open him up and do their study. His wife, Julia found him in front of the house on the ground after she came back from the grocery store."

*****

He would later tell Bishop that they had confirmed that she had been at the store when it happened.

*****

"No shit!" Bishop said, responding to Jenkin's

analysis about the killing of the man. "Damn." *Hate to admit it, but he was a perfect candidate to be shot. Pissed everybody he met off, big time.*

The chief made a remark about how that type of shotgun, a 410 gauge, was used for hunting, especially deer at short range.

"Glad you were at home. I needed to stop by."

Bishop frowned at the chief's statement about needing to stop by. *Why?*

The economy had been on an upswing so bank loans were mostly current. As a result, his help wasn't needed by the banks, so he was home more than usual.

Noticing Bishop's frown, the chief said, "I was in the neighborhood – checking on a sick deputy - and the sheriff asked if I'd take a look. I've seen more killings than he has. I'll give him a report. I didn't see anything that'd help though. He asked me to stop by and see you." *That's the second time he's said that, about stopping by. What the hell?*

"Well damn, come in the house and give me the details. I heard two shots probably close to twelve thirty," Bishop said with another frown.

Bishop left his tools in his toolshed and went upstairs to hear the rest of whatever Chief Jenkins came to say. He grabbed a couple of beers out of the fridge for them to drink on the back porch.

Chapter 3

Jenkins took a sip and said, "Big Jim, the sheriff, I think you know him. Anyway, I figured I knew you better than he did and wouldn't make you nervous asking you questions."

Stopped by to ask questions. What the hell is that about? Bishop thought.

"Well, ask away," he said. "I don't know much I can tell you though. Hell, I know about what you know. The guy was hard to get along with. Liked to throw his weight around. Fought with his contractors, once head to head. I think he intimidates his wife but that's my off the wall guess based on my visit with them. But she kind of stands up to him. Stopped him from getting into it with me, about Kathy."

"Julia told me about it, how he almost fought with you," Jenkins grinned as he said it. "Apparently he was making a move on Kathy at their housewarming party."

Bishop gave a half laugh and said, "Ah, so that's it." *Good God. Waste of time getting into that. It was nothing. Wants to know if I killed the bastard. Hell.*

"Kind of. The sheriff figured since I was a drinking buddy, you wouldn't mind me asking you about it. I didn't tell him how he'd pressure you to bribe the planning department to approve his wooden roof. I figured that was between us."

"I agree."

"But the face to face you had with the man at his

open house was known to Jim," the chief said. "Gossip like that gets around."

"I reckon. Well, it might have come to blows but Julia intervened. He'd puffed up like he was going to start swinging," Bishop said, and gave him the details. "I just wanted him to know that Kathy wasn't available. As far as I know, he didn't bother her after that. We didn't stay long after that anyway."

Jenkins nodded his head and smiled. "I wish I could have seen that. Watson was a tough hombre. And, if you don't mind me saying so, you ain't no slouch."

"Yeah, well, I'm damn glad Julia stepped in. He was a big son of a bitch and he looked ready to take me on. His way to solve his problems. Start swinging."

"So I've heard. And he was big enough to be the one standing afterwards. Anyway, the sheriff said there might have been some lingering hostilities between you and Fletcher because of it. He wondered if Fletcher made another move on Kathy and you put a stop to it, permanently," the chief said.

"Yeah. I figured that's what your visit was all about. The sheriff asked you to interrogate me as a possible suspect. Well, I guess that's logical. Even before he put his arm around Kathy I didn't like him. I didn't shoot him however. Not my cup of tea to go around shooting people, even those I don't like," Bishop replied.

"I told him as much but agreed to ask you. The other thing the sheriff asked me to do, if you don't mind, is to smell your shotgun. Can I do that just to shut him up about it? Have a smell? He said you can never tell who's going to kill somebody."

Bishop sighed. "Hells bells, Chief. Okay. Follow me. Don't you know that if I'd have shot the bastard, I'd have bought a shotgun out of state for the job and made damn sure it wasn't in the house in case anybody came looking or smelling."

"Yep. I know, and I told him that, but he said he needed to dot the i's and cross the t's."

Bishop laughed as he took him into the small room he used as his office where his 12-gauge shotgun was laying in its rack on the wall behind his desk.

"I don't have a 410 gauge," Bishop told him.

"Well that was kind of a deduction, as I said, kind of a guess based on the spray pattern of the shots," Jenkins said. "They may know more when forensics finishes up."

It would later be concluded by forensics that Fletcher was shot with a 410 gauge shotgun. It was also reported that the shot to the chest was the one that killed him. The second shot to the head was apparently to make sure.

Chief Jenkins took the shotgun off the rack, popped it open and took a smell. "Hasn't been fired in a long time," he said.

"Last time was three months ago. I killed a water moccasin on the slope out there. It was sunning itself but I didn't want to take a chance it might decide to slither closer to the house. So I shot it."

Bishop showed him the box of shotgun shells. One was missing.

"Yeah," Jenkins said. He snapped the shotgun to its closed position and put it back in the rack. "I'll tell the sheriff you didn't shoot Fletcher with that shotgun."

"Or any other, but I guess that falls under the heading of an unsubstantiated declaration by a suspect," Bishop said.

"I guess you got it in one, Bishop. He said he'd be damned surprised if you had, but he had to go through the process in case somebody looked over his shoulder next election and claimed he wasn't doing his job."

"I understand. I'd have done the same thing if I had been in his shoes."

They went back onto the porch where Jenkins finished his beer before heading home.

*****

Bishop told Kathy about Fletcher being killed and the chief's visit when she came in from her day at the library. She'd already heard about the killing, but was surprised to hear about Bishop being a suspect. She laughed.

"I'll have to watch you," she joked.

He took her out for a steak dinner just for the hell of it. It was a local place with a good reputation. They claimed to serve only meat grown locally. "Organic" they advertised with the tagline, "Good people eat good meat here."

They enjoyed it and the wine they ordered with it. Kathy's as usual was, according to Bishop, a paint stripping red. His was a mild pink. Afterward, they enjoyed the local favorite, bread pudding, for dessert.

Bishop had been called by one of his bank clients to check on some borrowers business, and to pick up their current financial statements. He was to study the statements in light of what he saw during his visit, and report back with any recommendations he deemed important to status of their loans.

He didn't see any major problems during his visits. A couple of outfits were a bit top heavy with overhead expenses because they'd hired too many relatives, mostly sons and daughters. His recommendations called for eliminating some positions so the business profiles would fit within the national profiles for businesses of their types.

Chief Jenkins stopped by a few weeks after Fletcher had been killed. He'd brought his fly rod to do some fishing. He brought a bucket and filled it with water for his catches to keep them fresh until he started home. Bishop joined him. Anything he caught went into the chief's bucket. Any fish Kathy served came from the fish market in town.

While they fished, Jenkins caught him up on what was happening with the Watson investigation including a couple of things Sheriff Thompson was doing.

"I assume you've been wondering what's been happening with the investigation of your neighbor's untimely end."

"I was about to ask," Bishop said, during a toss of his fly into the creek. Jenkins was reeling his in, shaking his head. The fish hadn't begun to strike. Neither one had caught anything.

"Well, the first people Big Jim looked at were the crew he'd fought with when they were building the house. They may have hated him enough to killed him after all their checks had cleared."

Bishop laughed and added, "Seems logical. I doubt they liked each other much."

Jenkins agreed while he was flicking his fly into the creek.

"No, they didn't like the man at all. Anyway, Big Jim sent his investigators out to question them."

"And?"

"To a man, they admitted their dislike of Watson, but denied killing him. None had a 410 gauge shotgun either."

"No surprise there, about the dislike. I don't doubt it a minute," Bishop said. He made another toss of his fly into the creek. He still hadn't had a strike.

"No. But the important thing is this. They were on a job, building a convenience center in Ocean Springs. That's about a two-hour drive from here."

He cast out his fly again. That time he picked a different site.

"One could lie and the others could swear to it," Bishop quoted an oft-used phrase.

"Indeed, but the owner had a guard watching over the job, a son in law. Wanted to make sure he was getting his money's worth. Also wanted to make sure nobody walked by and picked up lumber or anything else of value."

"He was there the whole time? The guard?"

"He was. Swore no one left the job site for more than ten minutes. Bathroom breaks. And when they stopped for lunch they sat on the ground and ate and nobody left for anything."

"So, they didn't do it. Or so it would appear," Bishop said. He had a strike and began pulling in his catch.

"That was our conclusion, mine and Big Jim's," the chief said.

Bishop pulled out a five-pound trout that he dropped into the chief's bucket.

"Thanks. That's enough for dinner right there," Jenkins said.

"Glad to help out," Bishop said. "So, if it wasn't the building crew who was next?"

"Right. My investigators, helping the sheriff, talked to all the women who have been mentioned in the rumors" the chief said. "Not only that, neighbors reported seeing Fletcher's car in their driveways."

"I imagine all of them had a story for that," Bishop said.

The chief laughed. "Oh sure. They did. Fletcher was there to discuss church projects. Religious visits."

It was Bishop's turn to laugh. "Well, in the scheme of things, I guess dipping his wick wasn't as bad a crime as some I've seen."

"Yeah. Hell, marriage must get old for lots of people. Probably comes a time when having beer with your buddies is a lot more interesting than crawling in the sack with your naked wife. A little variety might be welcomed by a neglected wife if an attractive offer knocks on the door. To wit, Fletcher Watson with his zipper down," the chief said.

"Yeah. Probably right. A bored woman might look forward to a little affection if their man has quit giving them any. Probably make 'em feel loved, especially if somebody like Fletcher, big, tough and handsome, comes along. It's a sin but only the Almighty knows about such sins," Bishop said.

"Anyway, we talked to all the women and the men. The women denied doing anything more than visiting with Fletcher. As I said, all were doing church work," the chief said.

"The husbands agree?"

"Most claimed not to know anything about the shooting or the … other. They all claimed to be at work or in their offices when Fletcher's visits took place."

"Any witnesses?" Bishop asked.

"Nope. But nobody claimed to have seen their cars leaving their work places."

"So, bottom line, no real suspects."

"That's right. You included. The sheriff doesn't mention you anymore."

"Any of them have 410s?" Bishop asked.

"Not one that we found. That doesn't mean they didn't have one. Just that they didn't have one when our investigators dropped by to check." He confirmed that their forensics people were certain that a 410 shotgun was the weapon that was used to kill Fletcher.

Jenkins added, "We also checked the gun shops in town. Not one of the suspects, that includes you, has ever bought a 410."

"That's a relief."

"Yeah, yeah. I told you nobody thought of you as a serious suspect. Just had to ask."

"I understood. Just kidding around," Bishop said.

Jenkins got a strike and began fighting to bring in a catch. It was a good-sized trout, over three pounds they figured. He dropped it into his bucket with a satisfied smile. "Some good eatin' on that fish."

"Find anything else?" Bishop asked. "From your interviews with the women?"

He shook his head. "Naw. Purvis's wife said Fletcher talked about Purvis's work. Apparently, his company had a government contract to make a computer system that's supposed to double the speed of a computer. I gather he'd overheard them talking about it in Church or something. Anyway, he said they should be careful with security. Make sure nobody walks off with one of the systems. He volunteered to look at their security if they wanted it. No charge."

"Nice guy. Trying to help out the husband while he's bedding the man's wife."

"Yeah. Strange birds in this world."

They fished another thirty minutes, talking between strikes. Both caught a couple more. None as large as Jenkins's trout, but in all enough to make a decent dinner for two. That was all the chief needed.

Kathy shouted down to Bishop who turned and

waved.

It was time to wrap it up. Jenkins was ready too. His wife knew he'd be fishing. He called her as soon as they quit and told her of their catch. He'd be home in a few minutes to clean them. From the smile that came on his face, Bishop figured that she must have been pleased.

*****

Bishop hurried upstairs to give Kathy a hug and kiss, their usual greeting. "I love you, sweetheart," he told her.

"Thank you, Bishop. I love you too. I hope you never forget it. You make life worthwhile." She said and added a second kiss.

They had their happy hour on the porch as usual. Bishop mixed the G&Ts and Kathy put out the nuts. He mixed his drink a bit weak to balance out the beer he'd had with the chief. And he knew they'd be having wine with dinner.

After the usual click of their glasses, Kathy said, "I don't know if Chief Jenkins told you or not, but there's a rumor going around town about the Watsons, well Fletcher Watson ... no, both actually."

"What is it?"

"I got it from a lady who works in Sheriff Thompson's office. The sheriff sent two guys to DC to see what they could find out about the property management business the Watsons said they sold before they moved here."

"The chief said he was doing that. What'd they

find?"

"Well, the interesting thing is what they didn't find," she said.

Bishop's eyebrows raised. He wasn't expecting that. "What?"

"No property management business in the name of Watson or owned by him had been sold in DC during the past three years. One business was sold four years ago but it was owned by a corporation."

"Could be the Watsons were using a corporation for the business," Bishop said.

"Could be. If so, it was apparently a Delaware Corporation. That was the one that was sold. They didn't find one chartered in DC, in Watson's name. The DC police are helping in the search for a Delaware Corporation with Watson's name on it. So far his name hasn't shown up on anything. And, nobody associated with the agency that was sold has ever seen or heard of the Watsons."

"May have had attorneys handling the sale. What did they say?"

"They did, but they won't give names. But they did say the Watsons weren't involved," Kathy said.

"Strange."

"That's what the sheriff said," Kathy agreed. "Nobody in any of the properties being managed by the agency ever saw anybody named Watson or saw anybody who looked like the Watsons. The sheriff's investigators had pictures."

"Could be they weren't using their names and had

people doing the work. Odd though. Somebody should have seen them. They probably had an attorney fronting the sale. But, managing a property, somebody should have seen them," Bishop said. "Just curious, what'd it sell for?"

"Five million."

"Enough to retire on down here, I'd say," Bishop said. "They have a local bank account?"

"They do, but it only has a few thousand dollars in it. Watson put money or checks from an Atlanta bank into it from time to time."

"Must have had a mortgage for the house," Bishop said. "The bank would have required a financial statement. That'd show a lot of their financial history."

"They don't have a mortgage. They paid cash for the house they own in Lawton," Kathy told him. "Used a check drawn on the Atlanta bank for the house. It's a corporate account. The money to build the house on the creek also came from the Atlanta account."

"Did they track that down? The corporate account?" Bishop asked.

"Tried but the attorney whose name was on the corporate recording wouldn't release the names of his clients. An attorney's name is the only name on the account. Fletcher, of course, was authorized to write checks. Maybe Julia was as well. I don't know if anybody checked that out or what difference it would make. They both probably wrote checks when they were building the house," Kathy said.

"The Watsons were secretive," Bishop said.

"Sheriff Thompson agrees but bottom line, he doesn't see any obvious relevance of their circuitous banking practices to Fletcher's murder. The property management company that was sold is doing very well. No reason for the buyers to want to kill Fletcher, if he was the seller. As I said, nobody knows for sure although it does not appear that Fletcher was the seller," Kathy said.

"All that secrecy sure as hell makes Fletcher's murder look suspicious. Must have had some secrets he wanted to keep secret.," Bishop said. "I have to wonder why he went to so much trouble to hide his assets?"

She shook her head. "The sheriff doesn't have any suspects or anything else he can investigate."

"So, case closed," Bishop asked?

"Looks like it," she said.

"We know they have money," Bishop said and added, "As you said, they bought a house in Lawton without a loan and built a house on the creek also without a loan. Hell, I bought mine from the money I got when I settled my suit against the developer and banker, but I wasn't trying to hide anything. The Watsons said they sold a business but nobody can connect them to the only property management company that was sold. What about a DC address? Has the sheriff found that?"

"No. No record of anything in their names in DC," Kathy said.

"A house could have been in a corporation's name, I guess. Strange though. As I said, it makes me very suspicious of them. Hell, maybe they were involved with organized crime. Big guy like that, He could have been one of their muscle men. Another possibility to look at. They might have left DC with money that wasn't theirs and somebody wanted it back. Could be they weren't really ever in DC. Wouldn't have left a record if they weren't there. Who knows where they might have lived?"

Kathy shrugged. "Don't ask me. That's more your cup of tea, Bishop."

"If they were associated with organized crime, that would be the end of the case. Those guys cover their tracks like nobody else."

He took her out for dinner and continued discussing the Watsons the whole time. When dinner was over, a link to organized crime was still the only thing that made sense, considering all the secrecy that surrounded them.

*****

Chief Jenkins came out a couple of days later, ostensibly for a beer, but as Bishop found out, he was there to ask a favor. Halfway through his beer, he said, "You know, I guess, everybody in town seems to know that the Watson's finances are a mystery. The sheriff can't find how they got the money they've used to buy a house or to build a house."

"I understand. What does Julia say? I assume he's questioned her," Bishop said.

"He did. Even brought the District Attorney with

48

him to do the asking. She said she didn't know anything about Fletcher's business. He told her he had a property management company and she believed him. He put her on the bank account in Atlanta, which she's thinking about closing. Planning to transfer the funds to their Lawton account."

"Convenient," Bishop said. "She doesn't know anything. I guess it's possible. She might have been afraid to ask the big bastard."

"That's what she said," Jenkins said. "She had to be careful dealing with him."

"Yeah. And she didn't look through his mail or go through his files. Not many women are that scared of their man."

Jenkins shrugged. "Just telling you what the sheriff told me."

"Has to be something they were trying to keep hidden," Bishop said. "And, I'm betting she knows."

"I agree. Sounds like it. The sheriff agrees too. That's why he asked me to ask you if you'd drop in on Julia and see what you can get out of her. They figure she might talk to you since you're not a policeman."

"Come on, Jenkins. Hell, I'm not involved in the man's murder. I had one clash with the guy but I barely knew him."

"He's not asking you to solve the case, just get some information so he can. So, will you do it?"

Bishop turned his bottle up and finished it. "Shit," he said. "Don't you think she'll know. Especially if she's not as ignorant as she makes out."

"Maybe. Who knows? Falls under the category of nothing ventured, nothing gained," the chief said.

"Okay. I'll do it. I'm not promising anything. Understand? Tell the sheriff that. I'm not a miracle worker. If he and the DA couldn't get anything out of her, I seriously doubt I can."

That's how they left it.

And that night when Kathy came out, he told her about Jenkin's visit and his request.

"I agree with them. If anybody can find anything, you can. You have … I don't know, a way about you. You can get people to talk."

Bishop laughed. "Come on Kathy. Be fair. When people get steamed up, they say things. Sometimes I get people steamed up. I don't expect she'll be steamed up. I'm just going over to have a chat. Then I'll tell the chief I didn't find a damn thing. That's all I'm going to do."

"That's all he asked you do to, sweetheart. Besides, he's your friend. A good friend," Kathy said and caressed his cheek with her hand.

"But it's Big Jim who wants me to do it. I know him but I wouldn't call him a good friend."

"It's Jenkins who's asking, Bishop. Jenkins. And he's your friend."

"I suppose. Yeah."

"It's the right thing to do. You know it. And I'm going to fix us some supper. The right thing I'm doing, and I know it."

"Good. I can't wait. You always cook some good stuff," he said.

She promised spaghetti and meat balls which was delicious, as always. He opened a bottle of red to go with it and even had some himself. He overlooked the taste and actually enjoyed it with dinner.

After dinner, they each had a piece of the pecan pie Kathy had gotten from someplace, with decaf coffee.

She told Bishop that one of her friends had a couple of pecan trees. She took a bag of pecans from their freezer and baked two pies, one of which she gave to Kathy.

Bishop was up early, thinking about his planned visit with Julia Watson. He fried eggs for them, including bacon. Instead of toast, he served warmed croissants.

After she'd left for work, he got dressed to drive over to the Watson's home. He'd decided not to call, figuring she'd tell him no if he did. A drop-in visit was likely to have more success than one he'd try to set up with a call.

She'll want to know why I want to talk, he thought when he was considering the options.

About ten that morning, he got into his jeep and drove over. They had a gate, like many people who lived in the country, but left it open.

He stopped in front of their house and got out. He'd only been there a few times while it was being built, and once afterward; the time he almost got into it with Fletcher. He didn't remember much of what he'd seen, so seeing it now would be like seeing it for the first time.

He walked up the front steps, and pushed the doorbell.

Chapter 4

Julia opened the door. Her eyes showed some redness. Her face had no expression but Bishop recalled that she was pretty much a stoic and didn't smile much anyway.

"Hello, Julia. I thought I'd stop by and see if I could do anything to help you through this hard time," he said. His face mirrored the sympathy of his words.

She looked down, shaking her head. "No. I'm handling it. I thank you for the card you and Kathy sent. It was very thoughtful." She looked up as though seeing him for the first time. "Oh, do you have time for coffee. I was just having one. Won't you join me?"

"Thank you. I never turn down a good cup of coffee."

"We have a machine like yours. I noticed it the day we toured your cabin," she said.

"We couldn't live without it. Fresh when you want a cup."

She agreed.

He followed her into the house. She asked him to sit down on the back porch overlooking the creek. She'd get them both a cup. "I use a mug. Is that okay for you?"

"That's what I use," he replied.

Within a minute or so, she returned with two mugs of steaming coffee and pastries on a dessert plate. Looked like miniature bear claws to Bishop. He and Kathy often had them on Sunday mornings when the library was closed and they could spend time together.

"How have you been holding up?" he asked.

"Pretty well, I guess. I'm always expecting Fletcher to be in the room. … He never is though. I guess I'll get used to it one of these days."

"Chief Jenkins of the Lawton Police force dropped by the house the other day. He said Sheriff Thompson was investigating the … well, the murder."

She looked down and shook her head. "He was just out here. I don't think they've found anything. Do you?"

"No, but the chief says they're still looking. He said the sheriff ran into some problems when he sent some investigators back to DC to see if your sale of the property management company may have left some ill will. Something big enough to motivate a murder."

She looked up. "He went to DC?"

Bishop nodded his head. "In a murder every stone has to be looked under."

"I doubt he found anything in DC, did he?"

"No, he didn't. He even had the DC police helping them."

She seemed surprised. "We didn't have any problems with the sale. Nobody was upset in anyway."

"They had trouble finding out who you sold your company to. They couldn't find it. What was the name of the thing? They couldn't find that either. The chief was wondering. Tell me the name of the agency? I'll let him know."

She looked at Bishop with a blank face for an instant then said, "I don't know, frankly. Fletcher handled the business. He didn't want me involved. You met Fletcher.

Well, you almost had a fight with him. But I think you knew him well enough to know he felt like he was in charge of anything he touched or wanted, including women."

"I agree, but weren't there records of the sale? Escrow papers? You must have had some evidence of the sale."

"I'd guess there were papers, but I have no idea what Fletcher did with them. He had an attorney. My guess is he left all the papers with him. He filed our tax returns as well. I just signed what Fletcher told me to sign. Didn't read anything. He would have had a fit if I'd tried."

Not many women would have been content to be kept in the dark like that, but not many women would have stayed married to an asshole like her husband. That reminds me...

"The day we first met, you said you were 'kind of' married. What'd you mean by that? Just curious."

She gave a half laugh. "Fletcher got all over me for saying that when we got home. I just meant that he fooled around so much, I hardly knew we were married. I don't know why he married me. Look at me. A plain Jane. Not many men would take a second look at me. I was working in an accounting office when he came in. A couple of months later, he asked me to marry him. I think I gave him a reason he couldn't marry all the women he was bedding. It made him feel good to think he could have practically any woman he met."

Bishop nodded. "Could be, I suppose. Let me go

back. Do you remember the attorney's name? The one who, I assume, handled the sale. I'll pass it on to the chief."

She shook her head. "All Fletcher's doings. If I asked anything, he'd have bit my head off."

"Well, I guess you knew where you lived in DC. The sheriff couldn't find that either. Where did you live? You must remember the address."

"I moved into a four-plex Fletcher owned. It was when he sold it that he decided to sell the management business too and leave DC. The building was torn down to make room for an office building, Fletcher said. Frankly, I don't remember the street it was on. There was a grocery store down the street. Vons I think. I'd walk down there and buy what I needed to keep house."

"Wow. You don't even remember the address of where you lived? Seems odd. Hard to believe, if you don't mind me saying. I can understand that you must have been afraid of Fletcher. I guess he beat you. Did he?" Bishop said, more in jest than anything serious but he did keep a straight face.

He was thinking though, *what bullshit this woman is throwing out. I've never heard such lying in my life. No woman would be that afraid of a husband. Good God! I bet the sheriff and DA must have been half out of their minds having to listen to this bull. I assume they didn't accuse her of lying because they didn't have any real proof, but they had to know she was lying.*

She half stared at Bishop for a second before replying to what he'd just said. Then, she sighed and said, "Yes. He did. The first year we were married, if I looked at him crossways, he'd slap me in the face and push me down. I got to where I didn't question anything he said or ask anything about anything. I was married and that was that."

Bishop nodded. *Plausible but still unbelievable. Totally. She'd know something. No woman would let her herself be kept in the dark like that. Well, time for me to do a little lying myself. Do a little fishing.*

"I saw a strange car the other day. Looked like it was coming out of your drive. I guess it was one of Fletcher's friends."

He stared at her as if waiting for her to explain. She appeared puzzled as if confused about what he'd said, possibly suspicious but unsure.

Finally, she said in a half mumble, "It was late. I didn't see another car."

"Well, you couldn't. You can't see the road from your house. I had just passed your driveway. The other car came out behind me. I barely saw it."

She nodded her head, sighed and said, "Well, it was one of Fletcher's … not a friend … a kind of business associate, he called him. I … well, I'd seen him before but I didn't really know him. He also emailed Fletcher, called a few times. They met about an old business deal. Wrapped it up, Fletcher told me after the man was gone."

Be damned. I may have caught something.

"Looked out of state, the tag. What I saw of it," Bishop pushed some.

"Alabama. He was somebody Fletcher knew from DC but he'd moved to Alabama."

"Son of a gun," Bishop said, "What was his name?" *She had to have been introduced.*

Again, she hesitated, looked out at the river as if trying to decide how to reply. "Uh, yes. Tyson Terry."

"What was the deal? The one Terry and Fletcher wrapped up?"

She shook her head. "I don't know. Fletcher didn't say anything to Terry until I was out of the room."

"I see. So, you were in the dark about him as well?"

She nodded her head again, agreeing.

More lying, Bishop thought. *Not a damn thing I can do about it.*

Bishop finished his coffee, lukewarm by the time he did, but that was not why he'd come. He'd come for information and he got a little. But mostly he'd gathered that she knew a hell of a lot more than she was telling.

He thanked her for the coffee and stood to go. "I'm sorry for your loss. If there's anything I can do to help you get through it, let me know. Are you going to stay here?"

"I will probably sell this house and the one in Lawton and move back to DC. I knew my way around there. But I have made some friends at the church here, so I'm still thinking about it. I could keep the house in town and sell this one but I do enjoy the view." She waved out at the river. There hadn't been a heavy rain in awhile so the waters were green and flowing gently.

"I guess he left you well off. The sheriff told the

chief that he … maybe both of you, had a bank account in Atlanta with big bucks in it. Was that in both your names or will you have to go through a probate?"

"The sheriff sure got nosy, didn't he? Well, the account was in both our names. I won't have to probate anything." She began walking him toward the front door.

Proves she's been telling me bullshit. If he'd been as closed mouth toward her as she's been saying, he wouldn't have even told her about the account, let alone put her on it as a signatory.

At the front door, he decided to tell her as much. "If you don't mind an observation. Seems out of character for Fletcher to list you as a co-signer on the bank account and a joint tenant on the houses. I assume you're a joint tenant."

"I am. After he'd met with the guy, Tyson Terry, he decided to put me on everything. I don't know why. Something the guy said bothered him, I think. I believe their meeting got a bit heated. Fletcher said as much."

"I see. Well, that worked out well for you. You ended up on all the assets you owned. No probate required."

"I am relieved about that at least. I just wish Fletcher were still with me. Even with our … conflicts now and then, we got along. I … I miss him."

Bishop thought she was about to burst into tears. But by then, he was out the door. She closed it behind him. He got in his jeep and drove to his cabin to make a report to the chief.

In his report, he told Jenkins that he thought Julia was lying about practically everything she'd said. "I'd guess she gave the DA and Sheriff the same bullshit she gave me. But there's no way in hell, from what I know about women, that she wouldn't have known the address of where she lived, or the name of the management company her husband owned. The fact that he put her a 'co' on everything else tells me he must have trusted her."

He added Tyson Terry's name and Alabama, where Julia said he was living, to the report. "She indicated that Terry's visit somehow upset Fletcher to the point that he put her as a co-owner on all the properties including the bank accounts."

If true, he reported, that would suggest that the meeting with Terry was not a friendly one. Maybe Terry threatened Fletcher. Bishop said he didn't see how, but it could have happened somehow.

"Maybe you should see if you can track down Terry and ask him," Bishop said to end his report.

He emailed the report to the chief.

Jenkins emailed back that he'd turned his report over to the DA and the sheriff. "I'll be out for a beer this afternoon."

Bishop replied, "I'll be here and the beer will be cold."

At four, Chief Jenkins' car pulled up out front and he bounded up the stairs. Even though he'd said he was coming out for a beer, Bishop knew he came out to talk about Julia Watson.

He didn't waste time about it. When the chief had his beer and was sitting down, he said, "The DA said about the same thing you did. The woman is either mentally disturbed or deliberately lying."

"She's not disturbed. I think she's hiding something. I'm thinking they were involved in something illegal. For certain something she wants to keep covered up. Maybe they used different names in DC. Hell, maybe they never were in DC. I'd run their names and pictures through the FBI channels to see if they have anything."

"After I gave a copy of your report to the sheriff, he had pretty much the same comments. He's doing the same thing with Tyson Terry, trying to track him down, if that's the guy's real name. Right now, like you, none of us believe anything the woman has said."

"They've got money. She does now. Apparently a lot from what I understand. I don't know how much, but they bought the house in town, no mortgage. And they built the house and bought the land next door. Also no mortgage," Bishop said.

"Just that will run to half a million. And based on your report and what the sheriff's investigation has uncovered, the Atlanta bank account has more. They can't find out exactly how much, but the banker didn't argue when the DA suggested it was in the millions," Jenkins said.

"Damn. Must have been some management company," Bishop said.

"It sold for five million. I think you know." The chief added their concerns that they still weren't sure the agency that had been sold actually belonged to the Watsons.

Kathy had told him that much from the gossip she'd heard in the library.

"Well, we have something damned weird going on. Organized crime or something equally corrupt. Otherwise why wouldn't there be some connection to the Watsons. You can't find a thing and she says she doesn't know anything," Bishop said.

The chief shrugged and said, "Yeah. A real bitch. Like we've hit a brick wall. Something's going on and we can't find it. But, it's a murder case so we're ... well Big Jim isn't going to give up and I'll be helping him."

"Well, keep me informed. If I hear anything I'll let you know."

"Do," he said as he finished his beer. "Gotta go."

*****

Kathy bounded up the back steps later.

Bishop asked if she'd heard anything more on the gossip circuit. She said she hadn't. He told her what he'd found out, as in very little, from his interview of Julia Watson and his conclusions. He also told her what the chief said.

"It is suspicious, Bishop. They must have over a million dollars and she doesn't know how they got it except that her husband sold a company whose name she didn't know to someone she also doesn't know."

"And, they lived at an address that she never bothered to know," he said. "And the sheriff can't find anything."

"And, everybody's thinking they were in organized crime. And somebody killed them because they took off with some of the … mob's money?" Kathy said.

"Looks like it."

*****

A couple of days later, Chief Jenkins called Bishop. "No leads on Tyson Terry, and the FBI doesn't have anything on any of them."

"Dead ends all around," Bishop said.

"That's about it. Big Jim is about to stop work on the case. He's spent all the money he feels is prudent and hasn't found anything. He did talk to Julia again. He said he was a bit rough on her this time."

"Did she cave in any?"

"Not a bit. She just kept telling him the same story. Even when he said they couldn't find any evidence that they were ever in DC or ever owned a property management company or ever sold anything."

"And you say nothing on Tyson Terry?" Bishop asked.

"Not a thing. Well, their search found "a" Tyson Terry. Lived in a little Alabama town on the Tombigbee River, Coffeeville. Sheriff sent two guys over to check it out. Waste of time. The guy was over eighty, bald and as wide as he was tall. Hasn't driven a car since his last heart attack. He said he didn't know a Fletcher Watson and didn't recognize the man's picture. His wife had died. He said he didn't have any children," the chief said.

"Bank I work for has a borrower over that way, Waynesboro. Borrowed money to establish two more hardware stores. One in Lucedale and another one in Alabama. A little town over the state line, Isney. Guy's been a slow pay lately. I may have to go over there and build a fire under him. The bank's going to try first. They'd rather not pay my fee," Bishop said.

"Good luck."

"Yeah. You check DC for a Tyson Terry? Maybe the Watsons knew him there and lied about Alabama," Bishop said. "Looks like they lied about everything else."

"They checked DC. Nobody had a record of a Tyson Terry there either. Likewise nobody in the FBI. And, I think I told you that none of the husbands on the list of suspects ever bought a 410 gauge shotgun from any of the gun shops around in the county or other counties within driving distance of Lawton or in New Orleans, Baton Rouge or Mobile. After that, the sheriff quit looking."

"I guess it is a closed case then. A man was murdered and no one did it," Bishop said, tongue in cheek.

"Yep."

"Big Jim asked me to ask you if you'd look into it before he closes it. Say for a five thousand dollar fee? If you can't find a creditable suspect, he'll feel comfortable closing it."

"I understand but I couldn't take his money. I know Julia is lying. Well, I'm pretty sure she is, but I wouldn't know where to start looking for a suspect," Bishop said. "Besides, my bank business has been picking up."

"Damn, Bishop. It looks like what I said then. A closed case. Sheriff doesn't like it but not a damn thing he can do about it."

"I guess not," Bishop said. "I wouldn't either."

The chief left and Bishop got ready for Kathy to arrive. He was going to grill some steaks for their dinners.

*****

The next week, the bank called Bishop and asked if he'd spoken to the borrower in Waynesboro about his loan.

"Already two weeks late this month," the bank loan officer told Bishop. "Was late last month too, and now he won't answer my call."

"Business must be bad," Bishop said.

"Tell him … well, tell him anything you want. I just want him to bring the loan current. The loan committee is on my butt. I recommended it."

"I'll get over there tomorrow," Bishop said.

The next morning, he was in the borrower's hardware store in Waynesboro by nine. He told the man the bank was going to foreclose on him. "They told me to take everything you own and apply it to the loan."

"Wait a minute, Mr. Bone. I was just going to call Jeff." Jeff was the loan officer's first name. "He's been calling me but I was waiting for a deal to close."

"I hope you were calling to tell him you had money for a payment. You said you were waiting for a deal to close. Does that mean you have money now?"

"Same as," he said. "I'm selling the other two stores. I have buyers for the Lucedale store." He pulled out some papers from a drawer and shoved them toward Bishop.

A quick read of the papers told him an escrow had just been opened to sell the store in Lucedale to a group of local businessmen who wanted to keep the store open. The borrower had been threatening to close it for lack of business.

"If I sell it, in a month, I will reduce the loan by over fifty percent and bring it current. I also have an offer on the store in Isney. Looks good. Should close in two months. I'll pay the loan off with that one. Make a few bucks on the side."

He pulled out another paper. "Here's the letter I was going to send Jeff." He handed it to Bishop. It was signed by the borrower.

"Take it to him, would you? And a copy of the escrow papers. He can call to see how it's going. I think we're all gonna come out of this thing in one piece. Please ask him to be patient."

"I'll tell him what you said," Bishop replied. He figured the bank would go along with the deals he talked about.

Bishop put the papers in his brief case. He had coffee and toast in a local café for lunch. As he did, he remembered Chief Jenkins saying the Tyson Terry they found lived in Coffeeville in Alabama, not too far over the state line. He checked the GPS to see where it was when he was back in his jeep.

"Can't be more than a thirty-minute drive. Hell, I can drive over and see if the sheriff's investigators missed anything," he said to himself. His thinking was that folks in those parts, maybe all parts, liked to name their sons after the fathers.

"Who knows? The man said he didn't have any children. Maybe he's slipping mentally and was thinking he didn't have any living at home."

Bishop decided to drive over to Coffeeville and ask him. He didn't have an address for him, but it was a small town so he stopped by the post office to ask. He flashed the postmistress a credentials card the chief had given him from another case they worked on together. It identified him as an 'Investigator for the Lawton Police Department.'

The postmistress told him exactly where Mr. Terry lived. It wasn't more than three blocks from the post office.

Bishop drove over, parked in front of the old house

and knocked on the front door. An elderly man opened the door. Bishop flashed the old Mississippi credentials again and told him he wanted to talk about his son, Tyson Jr.

He figured he might as well go for the jugular and get it over with. No beating around the bush.

"What?" the man asked and stepped back. "Who told you I had a son?"

Bishop bobbed his head to the right and said, "One of your neighbors."

"They wasn't supposed to tell nobody 'bout him. He told 'em all not to."

"Well they did, and I need to talk to you about him."

"Well, damnation," he said.

The man invited Bishop to sit down in a front porch rocker. He sat in the swing and told Bishop, "Tyson works in Washington for the government. Something secret. That's why nobody was supposed to tell it. He does secret work."

"Which government branch does he work for?"

The man said he didn't know. "The boy never says. He was just here not too long ago. Says he's retiring. Gonna live in Florida, he says. He'll let me know. Wants me to sell this place and come stay with him. He's buying a place that has an extra room."

The man didn't have an address when Bishop asked. Instead, he said, "Said he'd let me know next month when he sends for me."

"You say he does secret work. I think he works for the CIA. He ever mention the CIA to you?"

The man became blank faced. "How'd … how'd you know?"

That was what Bishop had come for. He thanked the man and drove back to Lawton. He stopped at the Police office and left a written report for the chief. It was in a sealed envelope for privacy. Jenkins was out.

"Please give Chief Jenkins the report when he comes in," he said.

She said she would.

*****

When he got home he sent the bank an email report on their borrower's plans to sell both hardware stores and pay off the loan within two months. He would later mail the escrow papers. The report made the loan officer happy.

*****

The chief called Bishop an hour or so later. "Be damned," he said. "How'd you find out? What gave you the notion? I don't know how you do it sometimes."

"I don't give up," he said and explained how it came about.

"I've given it to the sheriff," Jenkins said. "He's going to contact the CIA and check it out."

"Let me know what he finds out," Bishop said.

He said he would.

Bishop enjoyed a cool G&T that evening with Kathy

watching the peaceful waters of Indian Creek roll past.

He told her about his visit to Coffeeville and Tyson Terry.

"You found the man!"

"I found his father."

He explained that the son worked for the CIA according to his father.

"And, he visited the Watsons before Fletcher was killed," Kathy said. "Do you think he did it?"

"Could be. Question is, what connection, if any, did the Watsons have with the CIA that would have caused Tyson to have a meeting with Fletcher. Apparently a heated one, according to Julia."

"That is curious," Kathy said.

"I'm hoping Jenkins will find out and tell me. I don't plan to get involved."

"I don't blame you. From what I've read, the CIA isn't anything you want to mess with."

"Right."

Chapter 5

A few days later, Kathy came out and told Bishop that June, Chief Jenkin's wife, had dropped by the library and invited them over for a potluck dinner. Kathy turned it around and invited them for a potluck at Bishop's house instead.

To Kathy, that meant whatever she and Bishop were having, the Jenkins could share. In reality, it never worked out that way – with Kathy or probably any woman. Kathy always cooked something fresh for a "potluck" dinner.

"June said the chief wanted to come out anyway to give you the latest on the Watson case," Kathy told Bishop while they were having wine on the porch.

When they were almost finished with their wine, the doorbell rang, announcing the arrival of the Jenkins' for dinner. Bishop invited them up.

He opened a beer for Jenkins while June and Kathy went inside to scrape up something they could eat for dinner. They decided to use Kathy's variation on an Indian dish she called Dal and something she already had on the stove. It was made with rice, cauliflower and what Bishop called a gravy or sauce made of lentils. The sauce is what gave it a great taste.

While they were warming that up, Jenkins caught Bishop up on what Sheriff Thompson had run into when they went to Coffeeville, Alabama to interview the Tyson Terry senior.

"The house was empty," he said.

"Empty?" Bishop asked.

"Totally. The neighbors didn't know when he'd moved. They figured one night. The deputies were let inside the house by the local police. They found nothing that would indicate where the man had gone. And, the post office had no forwarding address for his mail. They assumed that the man would have put in a change of address for anything important, like social security payments."

"Be damned. Most people would have. I guess he talked with his son and the boy got him out of there before the sheriff could get back and ask official questions," Bishop said.

"I guess. The sheriff is fit to be tied," Jenkins said.

"I don't blame him. What's his next move, if he has one?"

"He's contacted the police chief in DC to ask his help to contact the CIA. He tried and got nowhere. The DC Captain asked for a couple of days to see what he could do. So, the sheriff is waiting."

"I guess the CIA only talks to the outside world when they have to," Bishop said.

"Apparently. He was asked by a lady who answered the phone who he wanted to talk to. When he had no name, she said they didn't do business with a member of the public unless they had an appointment.

"That's when he called the DC police and explained what he was trying to do. The DC Captain seems to think the police can make contact."

"In a couple of days?" Bishop asked.

Jenkins nodded. "Good beer."

Bishop agreed.

Kathy and June called for dinner. They ate inside. It was summer and getting hot, even in the evening. The porch had fans but they preferred the cool of inside air conditioning.

"Did the sheriff ask Julia what they had to do with the CIA?" Bishop asked during dinner.

Jenkins laughed. "Got another curveball out of her. She told him that Fletcher got a call from somebody he reckoned was the CIA about an eight-plex building he had for rent. It had great security. The guy he was talking to needed the security and wanted to lease the entire building. Eventually they bought it, she said and added that they were told not to discuss it with anybody. She didn't know for sure all the details and Fletcher didn't tell her anything, but she assumes the Tyson guy was here on behalf of the CIA to talk about the last payment they were owed."

"So, they sent somebody all the way from DC to talk about a payment?" Bishop said. "They could just as easily have done that by a telephone call. And I can't imagine the CIA asking for time or a discount that would have necessitated a personal visit," Bishop said.

"The sheriff agrees," Jenkins said.

"So, nobody knows where the Terrys are, the son or the father, and we can't talk to the CIA to find out," Bishop said. "Did he tell the DC police Captain that Terry junior is a suspect in a murder case?"

"I understand that's exactly what he did."

"Well, that should get their attention, I'd guess. Otherwise, the press could get the story and hell might break lose. CIA being involved in murdering people."

"I think he also told him that."

"I'll be interested in hearing what they have to say," Bishop said.

"I'll let you know when I find out," Jenkins said.

"I feel like going over to see Julia and ask her about it. Hell, all she can do is tell me another lie," Bishop said.

"Would you do that?" Jenkins asked. "You might find something. Last time you got Tyson Terry's name out of her."

"I'm thinking about it."

Kathy served pecan pie for desert with decaf coffee.

As they left, Jenkins said with a smile, "Let me know what the woman says … when you ask her about Fletcher's relationship with the CIA."

"I haven't said I'd do it, just that I felt like it," Bishop said.

Jenkins laughed. "When you feel like something, Bishop, you do it. Let me know."

"He knows you well," Kathy said after they'd driven away.

"Thinks he does," Bishop said. *Hell, maybe he does. I'll go over there and see what she says.*

Bishop rang the Watson's doorbell the next morning. Within a few seconds, Julia answered. "Oh, Mr. Bone," she said looking surprised. "What ... well, what do you want?" Her voice had a burr in it.

I guess I am a surprise. "I had a couple of personal questions to ask you, if you don't mind."

"Don't you people have lives? The sheriff is out here asking questions every time I turn around. And now you."

"Yeah, I guess we're a nosey bunch when things stick in our ... pardon the cliché ... stick in our craws."

She hesitated with a frown then shrugged and said, "Well, come on in. Let's get it over with. Move to Lawton and have a law man live with you."

Bishop forced a laugh and followed her to the back porch where he pulled out a chair and sat down.

"Coffee?" she asked.

He shook his head. "No, I just came to talk."

She sat down and made a gesture with her hands for him to proceed.

"My first question is this. We know you and Fletcher were CIA. So, no need to lie about that. But why did you lie about it in the first place?"

She stared at Bishop a few seconds. "Okay, I lied! Have you ever heard of the Official Secrets Act?"

He said he had.

"Well, we signed it and swore not to reveal anything to anybody about our relationship, even having one, with the CIA. So my only alternative was to lie. Fletcher and I made up the story about the property management company as a cover story."

"I can't tell you how much it sounded like a lie, to me and to the sheriff."

She shrugged. "Sorry, but I had no choice."

"But, if you lie about one thing, down here we all figure you lied about other things as well," Bishop said.

She gave him a dismissive wave. "Just ask your damn questions. I have work to do."

"One question I had was about your 'kind of marriage' with Fletcher. Why would a man like Fletcher marry you? I'm being straight forward with my questions, today. Tact is out the door."

"I agree. I'm a plain Jane. I didn't think I'd ever get married. I didn't even have friends. That's why I joined the CIA.

"That's why they hired me. I was a loner. I didn't know anybody I could tell anything to. And, I'll tell you about something else that seemed to trouble you. I was not married to Fletcher. My real last name is Florence.

"Fletcher came to me one day, about four years before we retired and proposed that we say we were married. That was so he could screw every woman he met and have an excuse for not marrying them. We told our bosses at the CIA basically what it was, so they didn't get bothered about it. It didn't hurt that I had some money. Inherited it from relatives. I was the last Florence alive. He also inherited some he told me. He got his from his parents. We combined it and put it into the Atlanta account that was always in both our names. We trusted each other. Don't ask me why. I guess because we'd worked together for years.

"We did that with everything we owned. Put it all in both our names. He did what he wanted, when he wanted and with whom but he never touched a dime of my money."

"So, practically everything you told me was a lie," Bishop said.

"As far as I remember."

"Okay, let's talk about Tyson Terry. Now that we're over the lying posture. Why did he drive all the way out here to see you?"

She sighed. "I don't know how he found us but they're good at finding anything. He contacted Fletcher now and then by email. Liked to bitch, I think. He must have tracked us down by our property records. Maybe the bank account. Who knows? Corporations don't mean anything to the CIA. We cut through that paperwork in a minute."

"So, what did he want?"

"He and Fletcher didn't like each other. Fletcher more or less got him fired. I think he officially retired, but Fletcher had let it be known that he thought Tyson was selling secrets to the Russians. Somebody was, and Fletcher had enough proof – his version of it anyway – to cast some doubt on Tyson. Tyson found out. That's why he drove over here to let Fletcher know."

"He ruined Tyson Terry's career," Bishop said.

"He did. And Tyson told him he knew. Said he'd pay

him back. He accused Fletcher of dealing the secrets. Fletcher threatened to kill him if he didn't leave the house. He did, but said he'd be back. He may have killed Fletcher. But I couldn't tell the sheriff because I'd have been in violation of the Official Secrets Act."

"You could have made up a story. Hell you didn't have any trouble making the other bullshit up," Bishop said.

"I suppose I could have. I just didn't think of it."

"I have to tell Chief Jenkins because we were just talking about it. He's the reason I'm here. We both decided you had lied and we both wondered why."

"Well, now you know."

Bishop nodded. "He'll have to tell the sheriff. I'm sure he'll be back for an official statement, not one of your fabrications."

"Yeah, yeah. Well, send him out. I'll set him straight. I doubt it'll help him much. I don't think he'll ever find Tyson. Nice guy. I liked him. He's a pretty smooth operator. Otherwise the CIA would never have taken him on. He'd been there since he graduated from college. I was a plain Jane, very plain as you can see. And there I was, butt to butt with knock dead handsome Fletcher. All of us started out of college."

That's about it in a nutshell, Bishop thought. *At least I know the answers to my questions. Still don't know who killed Fletcher for sure, but Tyson looks like a pretty good bet. Next question might be, if Tyson wasn't dealing secrets, who was. Fletcher had some money. Makes me wonder. Did he come to Lawton to hide out from Tyson or from the CIA? Not my problem.*

"I doubt I'll be on her Christmas list," he said during his drive home. "I wonder if she'll stick around Lawton now that everybody will know her history. I wish I had asked, but I'll know soon enough. If she lists her property, she's leaving."

*****

As soon as he got inside, he booted up his computer and emailed the chief what he'd found out about everything. Jenkins called immediately.

"I'm impressed," he said. "You found out the real skinny. I figured if it was there, you'd dig it out. For some reason, people tell you stuff. I guess you trick them somehow."

"It's my face. It looks honest. They think they can tell me the truth."

"Yeah, and bird shit tastes like popcorn," he said, quoting an often-used quip.

"I guess you'll let the sheriff know."

He laughed. "I will. He may give me a hero's medal. At least buy me lunch with County money. He may turn on his siren when he goes back out there. Scare the hell out of Julia Florence."

"He might have to squeeze her pretty hard to do that. The loud siren will probably only piss her off. I don't think she scares easy," Bishop said.

"I'll tell him that. He doesn't back down easily so it could quite a confrontation."

"I'd like to be there," Bishop said.

*****

That evening, as they enjoyed their happy hour on the porch, he told Kathy what he'd found out from Julia.

She smiled. "Jenkins knew you would discover something. I bet he was pretty happy that you got some answers."

Bishop nodded his head. "I guess."

"You always do," she added.

"I'm not sure about that."

"Well, you've given them something they might be able to use trying to track down the man's killer."

"If she moves out, I wonder if they won't just close the case. She's the only contact with the murder. With her gone, there'd be nobody around to care what happened to the investigation. Besides, it looks like the Tyson guy did it. Fletcher had cost him his career. He had a motive."

She nodded. "You're probably right. Even if she doesn't move, unless they can track Tyson down, why waste the taxpayers' money. Just close the case with a notation that he's the likely murderer."

"Makes sense to me," Bishop said. "And, he's … what is it they say in the movies? … gone to ground and took his dad with him. Who knows where they are? My guess is he'd worked at the CIA long enough to have saved a bit of money. Plus he officially retired, they didn't fire him, so he'll get a pension."

"You have it worked out," she said.

"A theory more than anything real," he answered.

"Well, our need for dinner is real. I better get up and get it done."

"I could take you out. How does a steak sound?"

She thought about it. "I believe it sounds pretty good. I've had a busy day and all this talk about murder and spies and killers has left me hungry."

"Well, let's go," he said.

They went to their favorite steak house for dinner.

"Great dinner, Bishop. I thank you," she said during the drive home.

"It was great because you were with me. Every time I looked across the table, I saw a beautiful and charming woman smiling at me. I could have been eating cardboard and it would have tasted like pecan pie."

And, the rest of the evening was great as well.

*****

Sheriff Thompson stopped by Bishop's cabin just before noon the next day to thank him and to let him know what Julia had told him when he interrogated her. He'd just left her home. He didn't think there were any hard feelings over the interrogation.

Bishop offered him coffee, which was welcomed. Over coffee, he told Bishop what he'd learned.

Julia pretty much told him what she'd told Bishop. And just as Bishop and Kathy had discussed, the sheriff was leaning on closing the case after an effort to find

Tyson. If they couldn't, which was likely, he'd probably recommend that the case be closed with Tyson as the suspected killer.

After he'd gone, Bishop checked with his bank clients to see if they had any work for him. They didn't, so he put on his work clothes and went outside to cut the grass. After that, he weeded everything that needed weeding and fertilized some plants that looked a little puny. And in the process, he figured he lost about a pound of the weight he'd gained from his dinner with Kathy.

He finished his work day with another cup of coffee on the back porch watching the beavers continue theirs. Then he took a shower and lay down for a rest.

As a nap was about to sweep over him, his phone rang. He was tempted to let the caller leave a message but decided to answer it.

After Bishop gave his name, the caller said, "Thank you Mr. Bone. My name is Aaron Todd. I … well I guess you could say I run a government agency in Washington."

Knowing what had been happening and what had been disclosed by Julia, Bishop said, "The CIA?"

"Ah, well, I'd just as soon not give the name if you don't mind. However, your guess work is good," Todd said.

"What can I do for you? My guess is that you're calling about the Watson murder and the suspect Sheriff Thompson is looking for, Tyson Terry."

"In a manner of speaking, yes. We were contacted by

the DC police Captain and told, or asked, to be cooperative with the Lawton officials. We are, for the most part, immune from such things but since one of ours is being looked at as a possible killer, we decided to cooperate in the investigation. That's why I'm calling you."

Why me? Hell, I'm not investigating the murder. He should be calling the sheriff.

But he decided to play along to see what the guy was after. After all, how many times would he get a call from the CIA?

"Good idea to help," Bishop told him. "As you say, Tyson Terry is probably a number one suspect in the killing of another one of yours, Fletcher Watson, I doubt you want that hitting the front pages of the national newspapers."

"That's about it, but we're not all that worried. I told Sheriff Thompson on the phone that we don't know anything about the killing. I got the impression he's going to close the case if he can't find Terry and charge him with murder."

Bishop agreed. "That's my understanding as well."

"So?" Bishop asked.

"So, why am I bothering you? Is that your question?"

"Precisely."

"We don't think Terry killed anybody. We know he was upset when Fletcher Watson accused him of selling secrets to the Russians. He saw Terry apparently trying to hide something, and told me as much. We investigated and did find the copy of a top-secret file hidden in his office. It was a study one of our agents had done pointing out weaknesses in our troop deployments in the world. It showed where we were vulnerable. He swore that somebody put it on his office to frame him. We knew, or strongly suspected, that somebody was selling secrets to the Russians. We thought it might be Terry when Fletcher said he was hiding something.

"We investigated thoroughly and couldn't prove that Terry had taken the file or made a copy. There was no record that he'd been in the file room in over a year. Not everybody is cleared to take files from the file room. Fletcher was. Julia wasn't. She wasn't cleared for the file room. Tyson was, of course. But we couldn't prove he had any contacts with anything else that had been sold during the time. But Tyson was so upset, he just resigned. He was sixty-six and could.

"You see, Mr. Bone, our profile on Terry is that he was a good case officer. Diligent and a workaholic. He stayed to himself. Unmarried and a very sensitive man. He couldn't believe we'd suspect him of doing anything that'd harm his country. He'd spent over half his life protecting it, he told me. He turned in his resignation and left town. We don't know where he is, and can't locate him. He's good enough to cover his tracks very well."

"Why tell me? I don't know him. I met his father, but I understand that he's also disappeared."

"But you did find out that Terry was CIA. Somewhat impressive."

"Lucky really."

"Maybe, but our file on you – yes, we have one – one that indicates you are a very impressive man. You can turn over rocks and find things and people that others didn't know existed. I wish you worked for us but you're too old to hitch up, even if you were interested, which I doubt."

Bishop again agreed. "I'm happy right here. You're right."

"And the banks you work for are happy. And I'm told the Chief of Police in Lawton, Chief Jenkins, relies on you to help him very often."

"I guess. Now and then we help each other out."

"Right. That's what we heard. So, the reason I'm calling… I want you to help us out. You'll get a contract from a company that does investigations. No connection with us. But you'll know. And you won't tell anybody, will you?"

"I haven't heard enough to agree or disagree," Bishop replied.

"The company hiring you wants you to find Tyson Terry and bring him in for questioning. He may know something about the leaks we've been having. At least we want to ask him."

"Big job. Like looking for a needle in a hay stack," Bishop said. "As you say, he knows how to keep a very low profile."

"That's right. He does. But we have to look and we have to find him. We don't want your sheriff claiming that one of our people, even if retired, killed one of our own, also retired. Newspapers would love to get that.

"And as I said, we're still investigating our suspicions that somebody is selling our secrets. More than a suspicion but let me leave it at that. It could be that with Terry retired, and looking at all the possibilities including Watson's murder, the selling of secrets may end. We sure as hell hope it turns out that way," Mr. Todd said.

"That might mean Fletcher was selling the secrets or Terry. Terry might have decided to throw the suspicion on Fletcher and quit selling. Or, it might be somebody else in the CIA who is thinking the same thing," Bishop said.

"Those are all possibilities we're considering. We've added safeguards. A camera records all entries. Agents cleared to enter have their fingerprints checked. Right now, we're keeping things open though until we find Terry. If he killed Watson, we'll deal with that also. We don't want him testifying in some way to get a lower sentence. The press would love that as well."

"I imagine they would," Bishop said. *Fletcher may have accused Terry of selling secrets to cover his tracks. Maybe that's how he got his money, selling secrets. Julia said he had some.*

"So, can we count on you to help?" Todd asked.

"Sorry, but I think that's way out of my league. And, I have work for some bank clients to take care of."

"Right now, you don't. Oh, did I mention the fee? You'll be paid two hundred thousand dollars a year in equal monthly installments. If you find Tyson Terry and bring him in sooner, you still get the two hundred thousand."

Damn. That's a damn good fee, Bishop thought. *Hell, I could take a crack at it for that kind of money.*

"I may have questions. Who do I ask?" Bishop asked.

"You'll have a contact at the agency. That person will answer all your questions. You'll get a retainer of twenty thousand. That should cover your initial expenses."

I think it will.

"I'll give my questions to the contact you give me. I usually have some up front, and more often than not, more as I get into an investigation. I might request some help as well. Something you might be able to do better or easier than I can. I'll be waiting to hear from him … or her."

And just like that, Bishop Bone was officially an investigator for the CIA.

Chapter 6

That evening, he told Kathy about the call from Aaron Todd but decided not to involve the chief until he had to. The chief might look on his assignment as conflicting with what he and the sheriff were doing. She was impressed by the call and Bishop's new "job."

"I'm not sure I can help them, but for that kind of fee, I'll give it my best."

"Might be dangerous. From what I've read, I get the impression that those guys act like the law doesn't apply to them. Tyson might have killed Fletcher Watson. Probably did kill him. Revenge, that's how it looks from what you've told me. If you close in on him, he might use the shotgun on you."

"That occurred to me also. I'll have to watch my back. Maybe that's why the big fee. Mr. Todd knows that too."

He spent the night thinking about questions he could ask whoever contacted him from the "company" Todd alluded to, his technical employer.

*****

A FedEx van brought him a contract the next morning, part of which was an Official Secrets non-disclosure form he was to sign and return with the contract. The cover letter allowed him to electronically sign and email his signed contract back to an email address.

With the contract was a check for twenty thousand, which went into his bank account that morning.

A name and phone number were given for him to call. He called the number and asked to speak to Jerry Rutan, the man whose name was given.

"So, Mr. Bone, we're going to be working together," Rutan said. "I guess you have questions? Mr. Todd said you would."

"I do," Bishop said.

"I'll answer them if I can," Rutan said. "Fire away."

"Do you guys keep tabs on possible Russian agents who buy secrets from our agents?

"Good question. The answer isn't so clear. We try. When we suspect someone as a possible agent, we watch him or her and anybody who deals with them. Usually they change their identities and move frequently to stay out of our surveillance."

"I was wondering, when you were investigating Tyson Terry, if you were watching anyone you thought might be buying from him?" Bishop asked.

"We thought we were. He was meeting a guy. Met him in a New York hotel once. A place in Atlanta and once in New Orleans. Turns out Tyson was gay and he was meeting lovers. Surprised us, because we thought he and Julia were fooling around together. Anyway, that was when we more or less cleared him of being a traitor. His meeting gave a logical reason for him being where he was, and it wasn't to sell secrets."

"I guess not," Bishop said.

"Kind of funny, before we found that out, as I said, we thought he and Julia had a thing going. Turns out they were just working an assignment together and had to be close. Of course, later on, she and Fletcher decided to hang out together. I guess you know about their arrangement … or do you?" Rutan asked.

"She told me. Pretending to be married to give Watson a reason he couldn't marry all the women he was sleeping with."

"That's it. The man had more women after him than half a dozen men. One of those guys. Amazing."

"I'd say. But getting back to Terry, send me the places he met anybody and the dates," Bishop said. "Did he travel much? Other than the three times you just told me about."

"Not much. He was sent on trips abroad but always with somebody, one of us. He did go to New Orleans again on a long weekend with his friend. Stayed at the Monteleon. They took a tourist tour of the French Quarter. Did that twice actually. And, he went once to Newport Beach, a conference we sent him to that time. He also met his friend that time too. Apparently, they were serious, may still be. We were watching him after Fletcher's warning that he may be selling secrets. But we never found anything that'd prove he was selling secrets. We still don't know how the file got into his office. It might have been planted. If so, one of the other agents may be a leak."

"Might have been Fletcher," Bishop said. "Thinking Terry was after Julia. He wanted her for his purposes."

He was also recalling Fletcher's conversation with Purvis's wife about the computer system his company was working for under a government contract. *Argument could be made that he was angling to do an evaluation of their system and pick up a system and sell it. But he'd have to be pretty cold bloodied to sleep with the man's wife and then steal a system they were selling to the government. But ...*

"We also thought Fletcher might have planted the file but decided he didn't after we investigated. But, getting back to Terry's trips, his friend's name is Fred Janson. Some kind of salesman. Not a buyer of secrets as far as we could determine. No known affiliations or products, just freelance selling of anything he could make a buck off. Travels all over," Rutan said.

Bishop made a note of all he'd said and asked, "Anything that might suggest where Terry moved his father to?"

"Not a thing. Isn't that why Mr. Todd brought you in? According to your profile, you see things other people don't see."

Bishop laughed to himself. "I doubt that, but who knows. I do get lucky now and then. And sometimes, people point me in one direction or another."

"Well, Mr. Todd thinks you'll see something we haven't."

"I assume if I need some authority and give your name, you'll back me up."

"Yes. I'll probably claim to be FBI. I'll FedEx you a phony card that says as much for you."

"Good. Probably need it. So, how about the senior Terry's social security check. Where's it going?"

"Apparently, the man never worked so he has no social security."

Son of a bitch. A dead end already and I'm still at the starting gate.

"One more question," Bishop said.

"Okay," Rutan replied,

"You and Mr. Todd have indicated that you know when secrets have been sold. How do you know?"

"Decent question. The Russians aren't the only country with agents running all over the world looking for information they won't have to develop internally. Anything, really, that gives them an edge in the so-called cold war we're waging against each other. As a matter of fact, we also have agents doing the same thing and when we get wind that something we developed is kicking round intelligence circles in Russia, we know somebody sold them something"

"Have you heard of anything kicking around since Terry and Fletcher quit the Agency?"

"We got word that one of our secrets was sold, a month or so after they both left the agency. It was a file that compared the defense systems of our top fighter plane with the offensive systems of the top Russian fighter plane. We considered that to be valuable," Rutan said.

"I'd guess. Anything else?"

"No, but it often takes weeks before we know," Rutan said. "I'll let you know if we hear of another sale."

"Good. And, I'll call you if I run into anything useful or need any other help," Bishop said before hanging up.

Rutan promised to fax Bishop photos of Janson and Tyson. Bishop got them the next day. They were remarkably clear.

*****

"What the hell am I going to do?" he asked himself after he sat down to think about the unknowns he was facing. "I don't know anybody to ask anything and I don't have a clue about anything helpful. Hmm, well, I guess I do have one ravel. Fred Janson. I'll pull it. It's a start."

Question is, how do I pull it?

After thinking about it for an hour, he decided he needed to see Julia again. *Could be she knows something that'll tell me how.*

"Damn," he said. "I dread that. Hell, she may open the door with a shotgun. I wouldn't blame her. She's no dummy and she has to be tired of being hassled by us country bumpkins." He laughed. He imagined that was how she looked at law enforcement in and around Lawton and the county.

He noisily let out a breath of air and said, "Well, she's not coming here to tell me, so I have to go there."

He was reaching for the door to his jeep when he had an idea. "Damn, I've burned my bridges with the woman. She's not likely to let me in the door. Maybe I should re-build a bridge somehow."

He walked around his jeep thinking then said, "I'll send her flowers. All women like flowers."

He pulled out his phone and called a Lawton florist and ordered flowers for her. "When can you deliver them?"

The lady said they'd go out right after noon. That would work, he figured. He'd drive over mid-afternoon. She should be in a better mood then.

To think some more about his assignment, he walked around outside. "I jumped to the conclusion that Terry might have killed Fletcher Watson. It might have been somebody local. Hell, men around here don't like anybody jumping into bed with their women. If I can find somebody around here that killed Watson, I think I can claim the fee without having to find Tyson. And the CIA would not have to worry about him spilling the beans to save his ass from a murder charge."

Problem with that is, the sheriff and the chief have already interviewed the men whose women Watson bedded. But maybe they didn't look hard enough at their alibis. Worth a try. I'll see if I can shake anything loose. Another problem is the sale of CIA secrets. I think they want Terry in their possession to interrogate him about the sale of their secrets more than they want him for the killing of Watson. Well, I'll take it one step at a time. If I can find the killer, I'll claim the fee and let them tell me why I can't have it.

He called the chief and asked for the names of the men they'd interviewed and told him, in general terms, why. "Somebody at the FBI wants a second opinion and one of their guys asked me to give them one. I thought I'd do a quick look at it and give them a report for a fee of course."

The chief said he'd have a copy of his files ready for him in the morning. "I doubt you'll find anything we didn't find, Bishop, but a fee is a fee, I guess."

"Is now and ever will be in my book," Bishop said paraphrasing something related to the Bible.

He had his noon coffee and a plate of toast and was headed outside to do some weeding when the florist called to let him know the flowers had been delivered.

"Well, I'll wait thirty minutes or so and drive over while she's, hopefully, still smiling. I doubt old Fletcher ever gave her anything but a hard time."

*****

As he left his driveway to drive to the Watson's home, he saw a white car – looked like a compact - on the road ahead. *It could have come from the Watson's home,* he thought.

It was too far away for him to see who was in it or the tag. And, he couldn't really say it even came from the Watson's.

A couple of minutes later, he was pushing the doorbell on Julia's front door.

It opened right away and indeed Julia was smiling. "Mr. Bone, I thank you for the flowers. They just got here."

"You're welcome," he replied. "I wanted to make amends for being brusque with you the other day. I was out of bounds. How are you doing by the way?" He thought it tactful to ask if she'd gotten over Fletcher's death.

She told him she was handling it better. She said she hadn't been up all-night crying or as depressed as she had been.

She looked at him and said, "The flowers are lovely. I can't remember anybody ever sending me flowers. In my whole life. It would never have entered Fletcher's one-track mind. He never had but two thoughts, his work and his women. To tell the truth, he was good at both from what I know."

Bishop acknowledged her comment about Fletcher with a shake of his head and said, "I'm glad you like them."

"Well, I guess you have more questions. That's most likely why you sent them. Am I right?"

Bishop laughed. "You nailed me, but that's only half right. I did want to apologize for being rude the other day. I was having a bad day."

"Come in and I'll give you a cup of coffee and you can ask your questions. It's not too late for coffee is it?"

He shook his head. "Never too late for a good cup of coffee."

"I baked some cookies. I get bored and do that sometimes. Relaxes me to do something productive."

"Good. I love a cookie with my coffee."

"Well, go grab a chair and watch the Creek run and

I'll bring the coffee and cookies."

Before he did, she showed him the vase of beautiful roses she'd put on her dining room table.

"I have to agree," Bishop said. "They are beautiful."

"They are!"

She gave him a spontaneous hug before letting him go to the porch.

He pulled out a chair and enjoyed the view until she brought out the coffee. There were no beavers at work on the other side, but the birds were singing, the squirrels were jumping from tree to tree, and the creek was running smoothly.

After a few minutes, she brought out a tray with their coffees and a dish of cookies. Napkins were already in a holder on the table.

He took his coffee, dipped a cookie in it and enjoyed the taste. "Wow! You did a good job with the cookies. They're delicious."

"I'll give you a bag to take home. I don't suppose your … oh, your fiancée will mind." She laughed and said, "I was about to say wife."

Bishop smiled. "Not quite. Kathy won't mind at all. I'll share with her. We share everything." He waved out at the creek and said, "Beautiful view. I get relaxed just looking at it. The trees in the background and the water rolling along. I can even hear the waterfall further down the creek." He figured that making small talk before he jumped into his round of questions was the polite thing to do.

"Me too. In the late evening, it seems louder when

97

all the other noises die down."

Bishop nodded.

She took a sip of her coffee, looked at him and said, "You had more questions. Let me hear them. I'll answer them if I can."

"I want to talk about Tyson Terry and his lover, Fred Janson, if you know him."

"I knew Tyson. We handled some assignments together. I didn't know his lover, but he'd told me he was gay. One time he hinted that we could tell people we were married to keep his preferences secret from his bosses. He wasn't sure how they'd take it if they ever found out. I considered it, but then Fletcher made the same kind of offer and, as you know, he was a handsome man. I felt a cover with him would be better than a cover with Tyson."

"How'd Tyson take it?"

"He didn't like it much but said he understood. When somebody planted that file in his office – he said it was planted – he withdrew from practically everybody in the agency, even me. He said Fletcher was trying to frame him for being a traitor. He accused Fletcher of being the traitor. Nobody could prove that either one was, but I think Tyson hated Fletcher after that. Didn't like him before. Who would? Fletcher liked to throw his weight around. A bully."

"My impression too," Bishop said. "I guess you get that way if you're as big as he was and as handsome. Women chasing you around."

"They did that. Women he'd run into would give

him their business cards and ask him to call them."

Bishop laughed and asked, "Did you tell Fletcher that Terry was gay?"

"No. I don't know if Fletcher knew or not. We never talked about it and from what I was able to hear, it didn't come up when they met. They mostly had verbal exchanges about who was selling secrets to the Russians."

"Terry was accusing Fletcher and Fletcher was accusing Terry, I imagine," Bishop said.

"That's about it," Julia said.

"Did you know that Fletcher had talked to Purvis's wife about their security on a system they were building for the government?"

She shook her head. "Well, he did say something about how he was surprised that a company in this small town had a government contract. Nothing about security or the system."

"Just curious," Bishop said and asked, "Did Terry ever talk to you about his lover, Fred Janson?"

"You've been talking to somebody at the agency. They followed Terry around after Fletcher accused him of selling secrets."

"Yeah," Bishop said. "You didn't answer my question. Did Terry tell you about Janson?"

"I thought I had answered." She looked at Bishop's face and saw that she must be wrong. "Well, I'll answer you now. Tyson told me about Fred Janson when he told me he was gay. That's why he wanted to "marry me" – to build a wall around his sexual preference."

"Did he tell you where Janson lived?"

"Not really. I think he was from Alabama someplace. Tyson said he had known him since they were in High School."

Bishop made a mental note. *Another trip to Coffeeville, I guess. May still have a relative around there or a friend.*

"Do you think Fletcher was trying to frame Terry?"

"I don't know. I'd told Fletcher that Tyson wanted to marry me without telling him why. Tyson had asked me not to tell anybody. Fletcher had been hinting about faking a marriage with me and I wanted to push him into making a decision. I think, in his own way, he was jealous. Or maybe he just didn't want anybody pushing him. The next thing I heard was that Tyson might be selling secrets. So, who knows? Even before Tyson was accused I had heard that that somebody in the agency was either leaking or selling information."

"The people I talked to told me as much," Bishop said.

"They usually don't tell anybody outside the agency anything. I guess you rattled their cage somehow. Anyway, the CIA also had Fletcher on their list as the possible leak. But they couldn't find anything specific to prove either one of them were guilty. Still, the charge upset Tyson so much he resigned. I think he had been thinking about retiring anyway though. The pressure of being under pressure all the time catches up with you. The charge just gave him an excuse to do it sooner."

"Wanted to spend more time with Janson, I

imagine," Bishop said.

"I suppose. Fletcher was upset that they'd let Tyson go like that. That's what he told me. I don't know if that had anything to do with it or not, but he said he was ready to retire too and asked if I'd retire with him. I told him I would. I had heard about Lawton and suggested it'd be a good place to live. He thought it'd be a good place to hide out if anybody wanted to find him."

"He said that?"

"Something like that. He said he wanted to live a quiet life. I knew he wanted to sleep with every woman around without having to show up for work every day. I think he had a hang up about sex. Once I suggested he should see somebody about it. I think he wanted to hit me. He didn't but he looked mad enough to. And he certainly didn't agree to see anybody."

"I'm not surprised. Did Tyson ever talk about New Orleans?" Bishop asked.

She frowned as if trying to remember. "He went there a couple of times with Fred. Loved it, he said. Said it still looked like an old French village, the French Quarter did."

"It does. Dirty looking. Kind of raunchy, like everybody is just there to have a good time. Take no responsibilities."

"He said something like that. Loved the coffee at the Café Du Monde."

"Anything else?"

She shook her head.

"He ever talk about any other places he liked? Where

he might want to live?"

"You trying to locate him?"

"Kind of."

"Sorry I can't help you. He may have given me a name now and then, but except for New Orleans, I don't remember them."

"Just curious. Did Fletcher ever talk about going on trips anywhere?"

"You think he was selling secrets?" she asked.

"It was put on the table by the people I talked to," Bishop said, and rephrased his question. "Did he go on trips? Did the two of you?"

She shook her head. "A couple of days before he was killed, we drove to New Orleans for the night. It was fun. As far as I know, Fletcher didn't meet anybody. We had dinner. Went to Pat O'Brien's. I'm thinking. He did say something after we got settled here about taking a trip to Galveston, Texas. I asked him why and he said something about a business deal he wanted to investigate. He was killed right after we got back from New Orleans, so that's all I know."

"Well, Julia, I'm pleased I have maybe become a better neighbor. I certainly enjoyed the coffee and for sure the cookies. They were great. I want you to come over and have dinner with us. I'll ask Kathy to pick a date and let you know."

"I'd love it. Just call or send me an email." Fletcher had given him their email address the day he'd shown them through his cabin.

Bishop got up to leave. Julia stood also and put her

arms around him for a big hug. "And again, I thank you for the flowers. I'll cherish them."

"You are more than welcome. I feel better. I didn't sleep much after my last visit."

"Well, I hope you do tonight."

"I'm sure I will."

"I'm looking forward to dinner with you and Kathy," Julia said, touching his shoulder.

"By the way, where are you from? I don't pick up an accent so I assume you're not from the South," Bishop said.

"Actually, I was born in California. Orange County. I went to school out there and took a job with the agency after I graduated. Both Tyson and Fletcher were already working there when I started. I think Fletcher may have been born someplace around Atlanta … or maybe not. I just don't know for sure. I might have said, Tyson said he was from Alabama."

*****

Bishop went home and wrote a report to his CIA contact, Rutan, who'd asked him to keep him in touch with what he was doing. Basically, he reported all the information Julia had told him. He asked Rutan questions about things she hadn't said or wasn't sure of.

Rutan wrote back and confirmed that Terry was born in Coffeeville and graduated from the University of Alabama. Fletcher was born in Florida and graduated from Florida State. He also said that Julia graduated from Chapman College close to where she lived.

"She was a woman and her degree was in computers. At the time, we wanted both. She trained our new hires, the ones who needed it, in computers. She also took cases, and was good in both. Looked plain as hell, but she was a whiz in everything but looks."

Bishop thanked him.

He also wrote an email to the chief to tell him how he'd made amends with Julia and that she'd told him a few things about herself but nothing, he felt, that had anything to do with Fletcher's killing.

Jenkins thanked him and told him the files he'd asked for were ready if he wanted them.

Bishop got into his jeep and drove to town to get the files. The chief was out but the files were at the front desk. Somebody had put everything he'd asked for in one file jacket with separators for each man they'd interviewed.

Bishop drove home and read them. He was looking to see if any of them could have left their jobs long enough to drive out and shoot Watson.

One guy managed a production unit at the local computer manufacturing company. Several people said they thought they'd seen him around the time that Fletcher was shot.

Be pretty hard for him to slip away and shoot the man with that many witnesses around.

The alibis for the other two weren't so fixed in cement. One guy was a real estate broker. His alibi was a clerk in a service station across from his office. He parked behind the little building that served as his office. The clerk thought he'd seen him that noon. He admitted that he was busy but was "pretty sure."

"That pretty sure isn't an iron clad alibi," Bishop said. He'd want to talk to the clerk again and then to the broker.

He had the same question about the next husband. He was a buyer and something of a manager of an electrical parts house in town. There were no witnesses who'd come forward to say they'd been in the store at noon the day in question. However, the store was open and no one else was working, so the husband, it was concluded, had to be there.

"Maybe," Bishop said. "Could have closed up long enough to drive out and shoot Watson. I'll need to investigate his alibi a little more."

He was also concerned that Fletcher may not have limited himself to three wives. Bishop wanted to see if there were others.

"So, I've got possibilities. The men folks around here love guns. And they don't like anybody touching 'their women.' I need to see who else should be on my list. How do I do that?"

Chapter 7

Durant Purvis was the first husband on his list. Even though people thought they'd seen him, Bishop wanted to be sure.

Purvis supervised the production unit of a local computer assembly company. Bishop asked the plant manager if he could speak to Purvis' assistant after showing the man his fake FBI credential.

"Of course. I assume you want to talk in private," he said.

Bishop said he did. So the man showed him into a small conference room and within a couple of minutes Purvis' assistant walked in. He looked nervous, as one would when having to face an FBI agent – even a fake one like Bishop.

Bishop stood and introduced himself.

"Farley Bush," the man said as he pulled out a chair and sat down with a loud plop. The man was somewhat overweight.

Bishop told him he was investigating the death of Fletcher Watson.

"Mr. Purvis was on the list of men given to me as someone who knew Mr. Watson. I understand you work for Purvis," Bishop said, glancing down at a paper in front of him.

The man agreed.

Bishop told him he was interested in what Mr. Purvis was doing around noon time the day Fletcher was shot.

"Ordinarily, he would have been in his office. He's in charge of the production of the computer systems that we build. He took his lunch at eleven. We start work at seven."

"Ordinarily?"

"Yes. But that day, he had stomach cramps after lunch and asked me to take over while he went to the bathroom. I don't remember the exact time. He called me on my cell and said the sandwich he ate for lunch gave him, pardon my language, but it's what he told me, he said 'the sandwich gave him the shits' and he was going home. I didn't see him again until the next day."

"Can you check your cell phone for a time?" Bishop asked.

The man did and reported the time of the call from Purvis as eleven thirty-eight.

Hell, he had plenty of time to shoot Fletcher and go home to nurse his sick stomach.

"He ever talk about someone named Fletcher Watson?" Bishop asked.

The man shook his head. "We didn't talk much, and when we did it was always about some problem or other in the factory. We build on contract. Right now we have a government contract we're trying to get finished."

Bishop thanked him. He asked the plant manager to have Durant Purvis come to the room so he could talk with him next.

A couple of minutes later, the man walked into the room. He looked more nervous than his assistant had. He looked to be in his forties, a little over five and a half feet tall and, like Bush, also a few pounds overweight, nothing special to look at. He wore a plain shirt and pants.

They exchanged introductions and Bishop told him he was investigating the shooting of Fletcher Watson.

"I've already talked to the police," Purvis said. "I was here until after lunch then, I went home and went to bed. Had a stomach problem."

"Anybody see you when you went home?"

"I didn't see anybody."

"How about your car? Your neighbors see it when you got home?" Bishop asked.

"I have a truck. I parked it in the garage and closed the door. I don't remember seeing anybody around. I did call my wife on the house phone to tell her I was home and why."

Bishop would ask Chief Jenkins to check. The chief was told by the wife that the man did call his wife but he could have done that before or after he'd shot Watson. A check with the telephone company would determine that the call was made after twelve noon.

"I understand you have a 410 gauge shotgun," Bishop said, bluffing.

"What? No, I don't! Never have had one. I have a 38 caliber revolver. I keep it in case anybody breaks in at night. I told the police that. They searched the house! I don't have a shotgun. Any kind."

"You don't really have an alibi. You could easily have driven from the plant to Watson's house, saw him outside and shot him."

The man was shaking his head all the time Bishop was talking. "I didn't shoot him. I didn't like him and I didn't lose any sleep when I heard he was dead. I think he was messing around with my wife. Pretty damn sure if you want the truth."

Bishop knew his wife was about ten years younger and physically, in good shape, from what the chief had told him. The chief had said, "She was a cheerleader in school and still liked men to cheer her on, if you know what I mean. Apparently old Fletcher was happy to do that … and more."

"Uh, the gate guard at the factory saw me leave. He knows me. Ask him."

Bishop would. The guard said he headed toward Lawton where his house was. If he'd been going to Watson's, he would have gone the other way. That was significant but Bishop knew that Purvis could have driven to the first road and doubled back.

He'd ask the chief to see if anybody on the street where Purvis lived had seen the man's truck that day. He'd find that nobody had.

"Have you ever met Fletcher or talked to him?" Bishop asked.

"One day after church, he told me he'd heard that our company was building a system for the government. I told him he'd heard right. He said he'd be happy to check our security system for weaknesses. I thanked him and told him I'd pass his offer on to my boss. Such things were above my station."

"So, as far as you know, nothing ever happened?"

Purvis shook his head.

After he'd finished his interviews Bishop went home and filed a computer report he'd send to Rutan. In the report, he told him that Eric Braswell, the real estate broker, was next on his list.

*****

First though, Bishop stopped at the convenience store and gas station across the road from Braswell's office. Fortunately, the store was empty except for the manager.

He introduced himself, again showed his phony FBI credential, and told him he was investigating the Watson murder.

"Police 've been here already," the manager said. "I didn't see Braswell's car leave. I didn't see him either."

"Were you watching?"

The man gave Bishop a blank look. "Uh, not exactly, but I keep a look out. You know, if something moves you notice. I have to make sure everything at the pumps is going okay. When I make that check, I also see Braswell's office and his car. He parks it on the side. He comes and goes but that day, it didn't move until around three that afternoon. He had some cars stopping by his office but as far as I could see, he didn't leave."

There wasn't a hell of a lot of room to second-guess the man, Bishop concluded. If Braswell had left, it would have taken him the better part of an hour to drive out to Watson's place and shoot him.

The manager might have missed him leaving, but if he had been gone that long, he should have noticed the car missing.

Bishop asked, "Did he have any visitors around noon that day?"

"I get busy around then. So I wasn't paying close attention to what was going on over there. All I can tell you is that when I did look, during the day, I always saw the car. Have to admit, if you push me, that the man could have sneaked out while I was busy. I just think I would have noticed if he had."

Bishop thanked him and drove across the road to talk to Braswell himself. The man was almost six feet tall and in fairly good shape. He was wearing a white shirt and tie with dark pants that matched the coat hanging on a rack in the office.

Bishop introduced himself as he had with Purvis and told him why he was there. Braswell also said he had already told the chief's investigator all he knew. He didn't kill the man.

"He'd been sleeping with my wife and I sure as hell wanted to put a stop to that. Too damn big to fight with, but I didn't kill him. I'm still not happy about it, what she did, even with him dead. My wife's at her Mamma's till we work it out. I probably didn't spend enough time with her. Preacher told me that. I'm thinking about it. I'm also thinking she should get her ass out of the house and go to work. Maybe she wouldn't have time to hop in bed with every Tom Dick and Harry in town."

"Preacher's probably right. Women think their

husbands should show that they care," Bishop said. "Instead they'd rather watch some sporting event."

Braswell didn't say anything, but nodded his head as if he was thinking about it.

Bishop said, "Guy across the street seems to think you left your office about the time Watson was shot."

"Bullshit! I didn't go anyplace that day. He made a mistake. I brought a lunch and had it here with coffee." He pointed toward a coffee machine near a table and a couple of chairs. "People comin' in like a cup and so do I."

"What'd you do with your shotgun. I understand the chief couldn't find it." He glanced at his paper and added, "I have a report that you did own one."

He came out of his chair. "What! Hell no, I've never owned one! Never! I have a rifle. The police saw it. I've never cared much for shotguns.. I don't have one."

"You could have borrowed one," Bishop said. "You must know plenty of men who own 'em."

"Hell, I don't know who does or doesn't. I sell real estate and play tennis on the side. I don't kill people even low life bastards like Watson. I don't know how his wife can put up with him. I understand he was tapping any woman willing."

Bishop agreed. "I've heard that you had said you were going to kill him. I assume you did."

Braswell came out of his chair again but turned to face the window out back. He shook his head. "I don't remember telling anybody that. Hell, I didn't want anybody to know my wife had been fooling around on me. I guess I'm a suspect, but I didn't do it! Look someplace else."

Bishop was convinced. *I need evidence. I don't have it, yet. And bluffing just ain't getting it. At least Purvis was out of the plant and could have killed him. Looks like this guy was in his office all day.*

The next day, he went by Lawton Electrical Supply to talk to his third suspect, Wallace Schrimshire, the store's manager. He knew from the chief's report that he often had help, during the busy times on Saturday, but hadn't had any the day Watson was shot.

Schrimshire was an inch or so over six feet, but carried a stomach on him and had to be closing in on seventy, maybe more. He had lost some hair and what he had left was white.

He admitted to Bishop that he'd closed the store at noon that day to go home for lunch.

"Frankly, I did it in case that bitch of a wife was seeing the guy. I had my pistol with me in case he was there. I have a thirty-eight. I might have used it if he'd been there. She finally got around to admitting it after he was shot. Bitch was crying half the day. Damn. I try to take care of her. Hell, I think I treat her right, but she screwed me with that Watson bastard."

The chief had said Schrimshire had married a younger woman, and that she still looked pretty good. She'd apparently been seeing somebody who was killed while serving in the Marines. She was pregnant and married Schrimshire on the rebound. The chief figured she told Schrimshire it was his.

"I gather," Jenkins told Bishop, "that she might not be totally satisfied with Schrimshire. That opened her up to assholes like Watson."

Seeing the man, Bishop had to agree with the chief's assessment that she might have been looking around.

"Was she at home?" Bishop asked the man.

He shook his head. "Said she was shopping. Hell, I don't know. Maybe she was. I had a coffee and a cheese sandwich and came back to the store."

The chief's guys got a "probable" sighting of Schrimshire's car by one of the neighbors around that time. The neighbor wasn't exactly sure of the time.

Schrimshire might have shot Watson and drove home so his wife could give him an alibi, Bishop thought as he headed home.

*****

Not a hell of a lot, Bishop thought as he sat down to finish his report to Rutan. *"Purvis looks good for it but I don't have any direct evidence I can point to. Son of a bitch. I'll have to drive back to Coffeeville and nose around. Maybe the chief will come up with other wives Fletcher was ... visiting.*

Rutan thanked him for the update and agreed with his conclusions – not enough evidence to recommend the filing of charges against any of them.

"Let me know what you find in Coffeeville," Rutan told him in his email reply.

Bishop gave Kathy the same report later that night.

"Well, it was a good idea and you did find some holes in Jenkins' investigation. That one guy, Purvis, could have done it," Kathy said.

"Jenkins said he's going to bring him in for a formal interview. His wife too. He hopes making it more official might scare them into admitting something worthwhile, by mistake."

"But I suppose you still have to drive to Alabama to see if you can find where Terry moved," Kathy said with a tired sigh.

"Yeah, I need to track him down. Also, I'll be trying to find something about where Janson might be living. I'll leave when you leave in the morning. I had hoped to find somebody around here who did it. Looking for Terry and Janson is like looking for needles in a hay stack."

She agreed.

They had dinner, watched something on PBS and went to bed.

*****

Back in Coffeeville the next morning, Bishop parked in front of the post office and went inside to see the postmistress he'd spoken with the last time he was there. Again, he flashed the old police card the chief had given him when he helped with another case. He felt using the phony FBI card would make her suspicious.

He knew Mr. Terry had left no forwarding address but he hoped to find somebody who might know something.

"What can I help you with, Mr. Bone?" she asked, remembering him.

"I'm wondering if Mr. Terry has any relatives left in town?"

The woman who looked old enough to have been there since the town was founded, shook her head. "No sir. They all died out years ago. Marsha, that's Mr. Terry's wife, had lots of friends, but she passed on … 'bout ten years go. Mr. Terry kept to himself after that. Hardly talked to anybody."

"Too bad. I understand that his son, Tyson Jr., had a friend that lived here. Fred Janson. I doubt he lives here now, but does he have any relatives still living here?" Bishop asked.

"Goodness me. I remember Mr. Fred. He was a strange one, was Mr. Fred. I reckon Tyson was about his only friend. He left town right after he finished high school. I heard that he went off to college someplace, but I don't think he ever came back. Now, come to think about it, he had a cousin who still lives around here."

"Do you have his name and address? Maybe he knows where Fred ended up."

She didn't know that, but she gave Bishop the cousin's name, Leon, and address and told him how to get there. It was only a few blocks from the post office. It was a small town and getting smaller, she told him.

Bishop parked in front of what folks called a "shotgun shack" with a front porch and two rockers, the standard, it seemed for such houses. It didn't look to have been painted for at least ten years. The roof was made of asphalt shingling. The yard was mostly dead grass and weeds.

Funny how weeds can grow but grass can't, Bishop thought.

One old camellia bush by the corner of the porch was bravely hanging on. The front door was open. A screen door kept out the bugs.

Bishop went up the wooden steps and knocked. There was no bell. Half a minute later, an elderly man in pajamas struggled to make it to the door. He was bald and his stomach had taken over his midsection in years gone by. His face wore a frown, reflecting his struggle to get to the door.

"Yeah?" he asked when he saw Bishop standing there.

Bishop flashed his phony FBI card and said, "I need to talk to you, Mr. Janson."

"Why you want to talk to me? I ain't done nothin'."

"It's about your cousin, Fred. He may know something about a fraud ring we're investigating."

The man began shaking his head and looking away like he wanted to run. "I don't know a thang 'bout Fred. Ain't seen him in years."

He looked like he was lying so Bishop put his hands on his hips and leaned forward to intimidating manner. He said, firmly, "Now, Mr. Janson, I'll tell you this, if you lie to me and I find out, which I surely will, you'll be charged under the Federal Aiding and Abetting Statute. You'll get ten years in a maximum security prison. For a man your age, that won't be fun at all! Understand me?"

The old man let out a noisy breath of air, looked down at his bare feet and mumbled, "Uh huh. Well, now that I think 'bout it, I may remember Fred being in town. Jes the other day … well, night. They stopped by here. Asked me to help some. I did. Fred, Mr. Terry and Tyson. They were moving Mr. Terry out. Tyson was saying he'd be better off with him."

Damnit. I bet it was right before the sheriff's deputies showed up. Damn. Bad luck.

"Where'd they go?" Bishop asked.

The man shook his head. "I don't rightly know. Fred just said something about New Orleans. Maybe there. I don't think he said but I heard him and Tyson talkin' 'bout New Orleans. Maybe that's where they went. Fred said I wasn't to tell nobody they'd been here, moving Mr. Terry out. I promised not to but I guess telling the FBI ain't bad especially if it's the law."

"No, I think you're right. It is the law," Bishop said. He figured that was as much as he was going to get out of the man.

"I ain't gonna git into no trouble am I? I tole you all I know. I just helped 'em get Mr. Terry moved. Can't do much these days. Got that ole arthritis in my knees."

Bishop shook his head and said, "No, Mr. Janson. I think you told me the truth. I'll recommend that no action be taken against you."

Bishop got into his jeep and drove away. He was back in Lawton by two o'clock. He parked in front of the police station to see Chief Jenkins.

"Jenkins," Bishop said when he walked into his office.

"Be damned. What brings you into town? Still working for the FBI? I wonder 'bout that, but I'll let it go."

Bishop smiled slightly and said, "I'm still earning my fee. But I need some info I think you and Big Jim can help me with, and maybe help yourself in the process."

"You found anything so far?

"A few things. Why don't I send you a report? Not a hell of a lot, but a few things you can look at."

"Good. Well, what big-assed favor do you want? I know it'll be big because that's the only kind you ever ask my help on," the chief said.

Bishop laughed. "Come on Jenkins. It's not that bad, is it?"

"You know it is."

"Okay. Have it your way. Here's what I need."

He explained that Fred Janson might know something about Tyson Terry.

"They want to talk to Tyson Terry if we can find him. Fred was Tyson's close friend. I've been told both were gay. They may be living together," Bishop said.

"Damn, you have been busy. I'm glad to have the info you have, and am looking forward to your report. I'll give Big Jim a copy. How do you think I can help? I don't know any of them or where they may be."

Bishop told him where he thought Fred Janson might

be. "Might have moved to New Orleans with Tyson junior and his father. His father is elderly. You may not know the Police Chief down there, but you guys help each other out don't you?"

"It's been known to happen if it doesn't cost a lot of man power, translated into money. So, what?"

"I want to know Fred's address, if he is living in New Orleans. While they're checking, have them check to see if they have an address for Tyson Terry, senior or junior."

"You think that's where they went to when they moved out of Coffeeville?"

"That's what I was told," Bishop said. "A possibility."

"Who you really working for?" the chief asked. "The CIA, I imagine."

"Hell Chief, you know I can't say. You know how it goes."

"Yeah. I've seen the movies," he said. "You'd better watch your ass. You mess up and I may not see you again. No more free beer for me."

"That would be a problem. For me too. Anyway, I know how it goes in the movies. If I say the wrong thing, I'm history. I'm hoping it doesn't come to anything that serious, but thanks for the tip," Bishop said.

"Okay, secret agent man," the chief said, "I'll talk to Big Jim. He can ask the sheriff down there to find out what he can and I figure the police chief in New Orleans will do the same for me. I know the guy. Even helped him find an escapee who was hiding out here in

Lawton."

"Good. Let me know. The guys I'm working for want answers yesterday," Bishop said. That was not the case, but it could have been. Actually, he was the one who wanted the answers yesterday but figured "laying it on the CIA" would give it more weight.

He drove to his cabin and careful to leave out all CIA names, he sent the chief a report of all he'd done since being retained.

The chief emailed him back a "thank you" and said that the Chief of Police in New Orleans had agreed to help find Janson and the Terrys.

He said Big Jim was doing the same thing with the sheriff in New Orleans County in case they weren't living in the city.

He then sent a report to Rutan about what he'd done that day, closing with, "I will wait until the authorities in New Orleans complete their search for Fred Janson. If they find him, I'll pay him a visit and no doubt find Mr. Terry senior, and most likely his son, Tyson Jr. as well. I'll let you know what they find out."

*****

That evening Kathy brought out some fennel coated pork chops for dinner she'd cooked earlier. She put them in the oven to keep warm while they sat on the porch with their G&Ts and caught up on each other's news of the day. She didn't have anything nearly as exciting as his but Bishop enjoyed hearing about her day just as much as talking about his. The library had received a new order of books. She'd saved a current murder mystery for him, had even brought him a copy.

And while they were doing that, they caught up on what Bishop's beavers were doing. It looked like they were doing the same thing each day, but it was always something different. Something new that had to be done exactly right to make sure that their pond environment remained safe and secure.

Chapter 8

While waiting for the New Orleans authorities to do to find Fred Janson, Bishop checked in with his bank clients to see how they were doing. With the economy strong, the borrowers were doing well and the banks were happy. They didn't need Bishop for anything. So Bishop turned to the next thing on his list, his orchard.

He had created an orchard area in the woods by clearing away small trees and underbrush to make room for the fruit trees. The area was one of those that was almost clear already. He figured from an old forest fire or tornado. All he had to do was to chop down the growth that had sprung up since the old clearing. The area got pretty steady sunlight during the growing season and his trees needed the sunshine. That's why he picked the area.

One thing he'd been putting off was building berms around his larger fruit trees. He had to pile a ring of earth about a foot high, around each tree so the water from his sprinklers would settle in and irrigate the roots instead of running off and irrigating weeds. The berm would also prevent the fertilizer he spread around the tree from being washed away by the sprinklers or the rain.

Some of his fruit trees also needed pruning, so he put the tools he needed in a wheelbarrow and headed to his orchard. He did the pruning first and piled up the cut limbs to burn later. He had set up an area he'd cleared for burning. Even so, he always stood beside it with a hose to make sure a spark didn't float into the leaves all around and create a brush fire that could reach his cabin.

Once he'd finished pruning. He grabbed his pick and shovel and began digging up the ground around the trees to make the berms. After an hour, he was well into the job and was working around one of his larger fig trees.

He had worked up a good sweat. It was nearing noon and he was looking forward to taking a lunch break. A cup of coffee on the back porch would be welcome. He bet Kathy was thinking the same thing. Maybe she would cut them a piece of pecan pie to go with it. He'd still have some work to do in the orchard, but for the most part, he was almost done.

It was Saturday and Kathy wasn't working in the library so she was helping with some weeding in a piece of ground adjacent to the orchard that they'd cleared for a garden. He'd planted the garden with vegetables she used in the dishes that they both liked.

He had enough dirt piled up for about half the berm needed for the tree and was digging up more dirt from a relatively high mound adjacent to the tree.

It was probably left over when a tree fell years ago and the root ball created the mound of earth which stayed after the tree rotted away.

Bishop was swinging his pick to loosen the dirt from the mound when mid-swing, a shot rang out and hit the pick's handle, sending splinters flying. Some hit Bishop's face with a sting and drew blood. If the bullet hadn't hit the handle, it would have hit Bishop in the face and likely killed him.

He threw himself to the ground as other bullets sprayed the area. He felt one tear through his shirt as he fell. He felt a burning streak where the bullet passed over his back. He rolled back until he was secured behind a berm. That kept him from being hit. Bullets thudded into the berm and into the tree but all missed him.

When Kathy heard the first bullet, she ran toward the orchard calling Bishop's name. Seeing him on the ground but alive, she grabbed her cell phone and called the chief. It wasn't his jurisdiction, but she didn't take the time to worry about that.

Bishop called to her and told her to get behind a tree. She did but finished her call.

Simultaneous with Kathy calling his name, Bishop heard what sounded like running in the woods. And, seconds later, he heard a vehicle drive away.

He figured it was the shooter's car and got up. As people do, he was nevertheless relieved that there were no further shots. He ran to see if Kathy was okay and was doubly relieved.

She told him the chief was on his way out.

"Good," Bishop said, brushing the dirt off his clothes and checking for any bullet holes.

Who in the hell have I pissed off now, he thought? *Has to be connected to the investigation. The word got back to the killer.*

The chief rolled up, sirens blaring and stopped at the orchard. It bordered the driveway to the cabin. He and two deputies got out to check things out.

Kathy was wiping the blood from Bishop's face with his handkerchief. He'd pulled a few slivers out and been dabbing at the wounds, trying to keep the blood out of his eyes.

"Anybody shot?" the chief asked.

"No," Bishop said. "Couple of splinters hit me in the face. Caused some bleeding. Had a bullet tear through my shirt. Missed me but I imagine I have a burn streak across my back. I felt it."

Kathy took a quick look and said, "Yep. You got a good one. No blood though. I'll put some ointment on it when we get to the house."

"You're one lucky devil, Bishop," Chief Jenkins said.

He pointed in the direction the shots appeared to come from. The deputies hurried into the woods. They'd find one cartridge shell. They figured the shooter picked up the others. They loaded Bishop's pick into the car. They'd dig the bullet from the handle in case they ever found a gun they could compare it with.

While the chief went to the cabin with Bishop and Kathy, the deputies drove the car down the road to see if anybody saw a vehicle on the road in the last fifteen or so minutes. Bishop thought he'd heard a vehicle earlier but was so distracted by his job, he didn't pay it any attention.

Many of the houses along the road were set way back from the road to be closer to the Creek so it wasn't likely any residents would have seen a vehicle. And they hadn't. Closer to the interstate, houses were next to the road, but those inhabitants were in town working, so no one was home to have seen anything.

Kathy ministered first aide to Bishop. It only took a few minutes. He ended up with a big band aid across his forehead and two round ones; one on his left cheek and one also on his forehead. She just rubbed some salve on the bullet burn mark across his back.

Then, at Bishop's request, she turned on the coffee maker and cut them a piece of pie while they waited for the deputies to return.

While they relaxed with the coffee and pie, the chief asked Bishop who he thought might have shot at him. He took out his pad and began making notes.

"I've been asking myself the same thing," Bishop said. "I imagine Fred Janson's cousin, Leon, in Coffeeville told him I'd been asking questions about him. Fred might have wanted to make sure I quit asking."

"How'd he know where you lived?" Jenkins asked.

"Damned if I know. But I suppose if was with Janson he could figure it out. Part of his job with the CIA was tracking people down. I did give Leon my name. But all that's more guess than anything else."

"I'll send somebody to Coffeeville to have a talk with Leon," the chief said.

Bishop gave him the man's address and said, "Must have been a good shot to figure on hitting me from the woods," Bishop said.

"Probably a couple of hundred feet away," the chief said. "Pretty far even for someone who's a good shot."

"Somebody with CIA training might qualify," Bishop said.

The chief's eyebrows raised. "Yep. You might be right on, Bishop."

"I'd guess the shooter didn't like the idea of getting in and out of the car … or truck, with a rifle. Might attract some attention. A Glock would fit in a pocket or behind a belt."

"Well, if we ever get an address for them in New Orleans, I might want the police chief down there to drag Terry … hell both of them, Terry and Janson in for questioning," the chief said.

"Hell, Jenkins, you know they'll say they don't have any weapons and have never been in this area ever," Bishop said.

"Yeah. You're right. Still, I want them to know that we know they probably did it."

Bishop agreed.

The chief finished with his notes. He'd give them to the sheriff for his file. Technically, it was the sheriff's case since it took place in the County.

By that time, his deputies had returned so the chief left.

Bishop and Kathy sat on the porch for a second cup of coffee and relaxed.

He told Kathy he wanted to talk to Julia about the shooting. "Terry might have called her for my address. I don't know if she'll tell me, but I want her to know that I suspect her. I'll do it tomorrow. Hell, right now, I'm too damned tired to do anything."

Kathy agreed.

*****

The next morning after breakfast, Bishop put on his jogging clothes and took a trail through the woods to the Watson house. One trail went along the river and came in at the back of their house. The other one, called the "inland route" by Bishop, came in at the front. That's the one Bishop took. It was shorter.

He saw Julia on her knees in a rose garden on the northern side of the house, the one with the most sunlight. She looked as plain as ever in work clothes. Her hair was pulled back and tied.

She looked to be weeding for the most part. Beside her was a pile of grass and weeds she'd dug out from around the rose bushes. They all appeared healthy, Bishop noted.

He walked over and said, "Julia. Good job. The roses look healthy and thriving."

She looked up startled for a second. Seeing it was Bishop, she forced a smile and said, "Thank you." She stood and asked, "Well, Mr. Bone, what did I do this time?" She laughed. "I imagine you have more questions."

Bishop also forced a smile. "I don't know what I'd call this visit. But I guess that's what I came to find out. What you did, if you did anything?"

"Shall we go inside or do you want to have this meeting out here in the hot sun. For now, I'll assume it's a meeting."

He shook his head. "Yes, you're right. It is a meeting. I have a question for you. It doesn't matter to me whether I ask it inside or right here."

"Well, ask away. I have work to do. Roses keep blooming no matter what the rest of the world is doing. I'll answer your question and get back to the roses."

"Somebody took a shot at me yesterday. Several in fact. One barely missed me."

"I know. The sheriff's deputies came by and asked if I'd seen anything. I see your band-aids. What happened? I told them I'd heard some shooting. At the time, I figured it was the bone-head hunters killing innocent animals. They told me somebody shot at you."

"Well, it was a bone-head hunter trying to kill me not an animal," Bishop said with a smile.

He told her about the bullet that splintered the pick handle and sprayed out pieces of wood, some of which struck his face.

"The shooter fired half a dozen shots before Kathy showed up and scared him … or her, I guess, off. The Chief of Police came out and investigated."

"I'd say you were lucky. Good thing you were able to block the bullet with your pick handle." She added a half laugh.

"Yeah. That's why I'm here. Somebody had to know where I lived. I've been looking for Tyson Terry so I assumed he might not want me to find him and decided to take positive action to prevent it."

She shrugged. "Nothing to do with me. He was here

the one time you know about."

"Did you tell him about me. Who I was and where I lived? Then or later."

She laughed. "I didn't really talk much to him when he came to see Fletcher. He hasn't been back. I haven't had anything to do with him since we worked together at the agency."

"He might have called," Bishop said.

"Why, to find out about you? If he wanted to find you, he wouldn't need to ask me."

"I assumed that'd be the case, but I figured it'd be easier than undertaking one of his CIA searches. I don't even know, now that he's retired, if he has access to the information bases he'd need to track me down."

"I don't either and I don't care, Mr. Bone. You're not my problem." She waved at her roses. "They are my problem."

"If you've been telling people, mainly Tyson, how to find me, and I turn up dead, you can bet the police and sheriff will be out here looking to arrest you for conspiracy to commit murder. The police have the bullet that splintered the pick handle. If they find Terry and he has a Glock that matches up, he'll spend some time in Parchman. And if I'm dead, he'll be sitting in that chair, the one he'll have to be lifted out of."

"If you turn up dead, let 'em come. They won't be able to nail me for anything. I didn't shoot at you. I was having coffee with some church ladies. Okay?" She turned her back on Bishop and dropped to her knees to resume weeding the rose bed.

"Church ladies. I don't guess the preacher came with them?" Bishop asked.

She looked up and said, "No, the preacher didn't. It was a ladies meeting, a private get together. We want to raise money to help a family having a hard time."

Bishop couldn't really tell if she was lying or not. *She's a cold bloodied woman though. I guess that's how she got along with Fletcher. I sure as hell wouldn't put it past her to give Terry my address, but she's not going to tell me shit. Church ladies. I wonder if that included the ladies Fletcher visited. I doubt they'd want to face the man's wife.*

He took the trail back to his cabin.

He told Kathy what he'd found out – nothing – and wrote the chief a report. He also wrote a separate report to Rutan to let him know that he'd been shot at. Hit by splinters, he'd said to embellish the attack. He told him he'd suspected Julia might have given Terry his address but he wasn't able to get her to admit anything.

"So I'm still waiting for something from the Chief of Police in New Orleans or the sheriff. If they find Janson and the others, I'll pay them a visit and see what I can shake out of them. I'm assuming they'll be in custody so I can question them in a jail cell."

Rutan wrote back and thanked him for the report and said he was sorry about the shooting. "It happens to our guys in the field quite often. Sorry it happened to you. We learn to watch our backs. I guess you'll be learning that as well."

Hell, I learned that years ago. I watch mine. I just

didn't figure anybody would sneak up behind me in the woods and try to take me out. Terry has to be the logical choice if he had anything to do with killing Fletcher. Right now, he's at the top of my suspect list.

I wonder if the chief had any luck following up on my suspicions about the two husbands who had axes to grind with Fletcher about their wives. Their alibis weren't all that solid.

He'd ask next week. Just then, he had the rest of Sunday he wanted to enjoy with Kathy.

She'd finished vacuuming the cabin, something she did during the weekends she spent with him. "You never seem to see the dust or dirt," she often told him.

"It has to be big to get my attention," he answered.

"You can leave tracks in it now," she'd said. "Look behind you."

He laughed.

*****

A few days later the chief called to tell him that they couldn't find Leon in Coffeeville. He apparently hadn't moved, but wasn't at home and the neighbors didn't know where he was.

He gave Bishop their final report on the attempt to kill him in the orchard.

"Somebody most likely shot at you with an automatic hand gun. We're pretty sure that the spent cartridge we found was ejected from a Glock. Good thing the shooter didn't use a rifle, or you might be dead."

*****

Monday came right on cue. Kathy got dressed while Bishop put a breakfast together. He didn't have a schedule so he didn't have to get dressed. In fact, he didn't have anything scheduled.

I hope a bank calls with a problem, he thought as he fried their eggs. The bacon was frying itself in a bacon cooker he'd bought.

After she'd gone, he got dressed and looked at the notes he'd been accumulating on the Fletcher murder. Nothing revealing jumped into his thoughts.

I can't just go to the French Quarter and start knocking on doors. That's where he figured Janson and Tyson and senior ended up. He doubted they'd feel comfortable in the upscale Garden District, having been raised in small town Coffeeville, Alabama.

But who knows? he asked himself. *Maybe they want to put on the dog.* He doubted it however. The French Quarter was the place they'd want to be. Entertainment was right around every corner. Restaurants and anything else they wanted was available for a price.

"I guess Janson is still selling his goods. Has to have money to live on. I wonder what Tyson is doing with his time? I guess he gets money from the CIA, his retirement. I wonder where his checks are sent. Probably deposited in a bank and forwarded to a post office box. His father apparently has learned to accept a leisurely

134

pace of life and live on whatever his son sends his way."

He sent Rutan an email asking if he had followed up on Terry's checks. The reply came right away. They had followed up. The checks went to an Atlanta bank. Terry apparently used outside terminals near the bank's branches all around the state to withdraw cash.

He figured Terry might have another account someplace under a corporate name. They hadn't found one but that was a possibility. Another possible scenario had Terry exchanging cash for checks from Janson. He could then deposit Janson's checks in his corporate account and nobody could trace them.

Jerry decided that Janson had long ago established a corporate checking account for his activities. And the CIA, thus far, hadn't discovered its name or where it was but they were still looking.

*****

Bishop sighed. "Come on New Orleans police. Find me an address."

He called the preacher at the church the Watson's attended and asked if the ladies had a meeting at Julia Florence's home to discuss raising money for a needy family. He gave the man his cover story, how he was working for the FBI investigating the murder of Fletcher Watson.

"The meeting might have no bearing on his murder, but I've been instructed to follow up on anything that happens to the Watson family."

135

The preacher, whose name was Walter Anderson, hesitated for a second before replying. "I can't say I've heard about a needy family or a fund raiser. That doesn't mean it didn't happen, just that nobody told me about it."

"Do they usually?" Bishop asked.

"Well, yes they do. The church likes to give its blessings to such activities. We put something in the Sunday bulletin to bring notice to it. We like to reward such good doings," the preacher said.

"Would you ask around for me? I'm working with the FBI and I need to know who I can trust and who I can't."

He said he would. "I'll let you know."

Bishop thanked him and ended the call. *So, Julia was lying or they hadn't reported the meeting or the fund-raising project to the preacher.*

He was about to call the chief to see if the New Orleans police or sheriff's department had found Janson or the Terrys but remembered something he wanted to ask the preacher. So, he delayed his call to the chief and called the preacher back.

"Preacher Anderson," Bishop said. "This is Bishop Bone again. I had another question I needed to ask. Chief Jenkins may have already asked. If so, I can get your answer from him."

"Uh, well, ask it. I'll tell you if I can," the preacher said. His voice carried a nervous tone.

"I'm sure you know or have been told since Fletcher Watson was killed while … let me say it this way, while

136

he was sleeping with a number of married women in the church."

"Yes. I've heard about it. Disgraceful," the preacher said. "A violation of God's laws."

"No doubt. We've been told about three ladies who fell under Mr. Watson's spell. I suspect there were others. And that brings me to my question. Could you give me their names? We need to talk to their husbands to see if they, well, killed the man."

"I can't tell you that, Mr. Bone. It would be a violation of something I was told in confidence."

"Well, Preacher Anderson, if you don't, the names of the other ladies could be released to the press. How would you like that? Your church being exposed like that."

"You mean you'd do that?"

"I wouldn't have a choice. But if you tell me the names, you can be certain I'll never tell anybody how I came by them. That kind of information is usually kicked around in gossip. Relatively easy to find. I'm just trying to save time and money by asking you."

There was silence in Bishop's phone.

Finally, Bishop asked, "Are you still there, Preacher?"

"Uh, yes. I just had to go into my office for privacy. I'm going to give you two names but I will only do that if you promise not to reveal how you came by them."

"Not a problem. The FBI has ways to find these things out. Everybody knows that."

The preacher gave him two names. Both were

lawyers. He'd counseled both and their wives. It appeared that they were going to work things out and stay together. "If you reveal their names to the public, that could very well be a disaster in light of the counseling I've had with the parties."

Only if one of them didn't kill the very busy Mr. Watson.

"No worry, Mr. Anderson. It'll never be revealed … unless one of them is a killer."

"I understand."

*****

Bishop was about to call the chief but the chief called him first.

"Bishop," he said. "Thought you might want a report from New Orleans."

"I was about to call you," Bishop said.

"How about that. Be damned, you've become clairvoyant now. Well, I'm afraid I don't have much news. They haven't found Janson or the Terrys. If they're living down there, they might be using fictitious names."

"Damn. I must be barking up with wrong tree. Maybe Leon gave me a bum steer or maybe he just told me what he knew and that wasn't worth a damn."

"I don't know. Could be. But they aren't giving up. They figure if Janson moved the Terrys into New Orleans recently, somebody would know about it. So, they're hitting all the brokers in town about recent move-ins. Let's see what that buys us."

"Good idea. I hope it pays off."

"Me too. We still want to find out who killed Watson. I know you're after them for … your client. Who knows what they want to do? I don't care. If we get the killer first, hell will have to freeze over before we give him up."

"I understand they can make hell freeze over," Bishop said.

"We'll see," the chief said. "I'll let you know what they find out."

"If they find out anything," Bishop said.

"I understand what you're saying. So, why were you about to call me?"

Bishop gave him the names of the two lawyers the preacher had given him and the preacher's concern about the names being made public.

"I don't blame him. He's patched things up and he wants them to stay that way."

Bishop asked if he could very discreetly see if they had alibis. "Why not do it yourself? No way for it to leak out if you do it."

He agreed and would get on it the next morning.

*****

Dinner with Kathy was a bit glum. The news out of New Orleans wasn't uplifting. He'd hoped for better results. The broad-brush search they were about to do would take time, he figured and Rutan would be wondering what the hell his high paid investigator was doing for his money.

At least he'd been able to pull off his band-aids. He was almost healed. And, his back had quit itching so bad he had to sleep on one side or the other. He did his best thinking laying on his back so finding a way to sleep in bed without itching was an improvement. Unfortunately, he hadn't come up with anything while he was laying there thinking that would help him with his problem.

After his conversation with the chief, he'd sent Rutan a report. It was more glowing than he felt. He'd said the Police Chief in New Orleans had had good results searching for people using the approach he'd outlined to Jenkins. He also told him about the two additional suspects they had. "Both lawyers," Bishop said.

He ended his report on a positive note. "I expect good results within a day or two."

Jerry sent a reply thanking him for his work.

He didn't feel positive at all and his dinner with Kathy wasn't its usual happy affair. She'd brought out a pizza. He liked it, but wished he could have been more fun.

She said she understood. "I've had days like that," she said.

He thanked her for understanding.

The next morning, he was feeling better. *Hell, if New Orleans can't find them, I'll just have to sit down and come up with another plan.*

Waiting for news, he cleaned all the garden beds of

all weeds, pruned any branch that looked like it was going to crowd in where it wasn't wanted, cut the grass around the house and fertilized any plant or tree that appeared to need a bite of something nourishing. And, taking Kathy's suggestion to heart, he even vacuumed the house.

"Can't see my tracks now," he said when he'd finished.

The chief called him a few minutes after lunch to give him an update on the two lawyers.

"Well, here it is," he said and told him what he'd found out when he personally investigated the movements of the two lawyers the day Watson was killed.

The first lawyer was in trial that day. He took a lunch break and had a sandwich and coffee for lunch at a café across the street. There were plenty of witnesses so he couldn't have done it.

The second lawyer was in conference with clients beginning a few minutes after eleven. The meeting, with a break for lunch that they had in the conference room, lasted until a few minutes before one.

The conference was about a corporation a husband and wife wanted to form for an upscale bistro in town where the well-to-do could meet for a glass of wine and hors d'oeuvres and just relax after a hard day. If successful, they planned to open a chain in other small towns.

"So," Bishop said. "Not a damn thing that'll do any of us any good."

"'Fraid not," the chief said glumly. "Good find though. You never fail to amaze me with what you dig up."

"Thanks, Chief, but what I want is to find something decent that'll tell me who did it."

"I understand, Bishop, and I have every expectation that you'll find it."

"Yeah."

Bishop had a cup of coffee on the porch and watched the beavers work. And he cursed at his frustration.

"No damn news," he said. "Maybe there's no news to be found."

But he wouldn't have to wait forever to get some. He'd get some news that'd cheer him up the next week just before he was about to go out of his gourd from boredom. It wasn't much, but it was more than the nothing he'd been getting.

Chapter 9

Bishop's phone rang shortly after Kathy had left for the library. He was already pondering what he was going to do that day. His investigation seemed to be going nowhere.

"Hello," he answered. "Bone."

"Bone," Chief Jenkins replied, tongue in cheek. "I have some news for you. New Orleans news and it's not too bad. Or totally good. Nothing with names, that's a problem, but I don't think you'll need 'em. You know them. Anyway, I just got a call from Police Chief Allerman in New Orleans and guess what?"

"I'm guessing," Bishop said. "What?"

"A broker reported just renting a three bedroom place on the fringes of the French Quarter to, get this, three guys. Place had just been rehabbed. One old guy who looked wobbly and about to cash in his chips."

"The elderly Terry," Bishop interrupted to say.

"My thought too," Jenkins said. "The other two men who called themselves, Tom and Jerry, appeared very friendly, the broker said. I guess you can deduce what he meant."

Tom and Jerry. Be damned. I'll tell Rutan they're using his name.

"I can. They like each other," Bishop said with a smile.

"Yeah. Anyway, the one guy paid the rent with a corporate check."

Janson most likely, using his corporation. I'll want the name from the broker to make sure, Bishop thought.

The chief gave him the broker's name and phone number.

"I'd better get down there today," Bishop said. "Both those guys are savvy enough to know the CIA is looking for them. I'm betting they're establishing, or already have, a contact within the police department to keep them informed."

"Damn, I agree. Hadn't thought of it, but I bet you're right," Jenkins said.

Bishop hung up and sent Rutan an email telling him what Jenkins had just reported including the use of Tom and Jerry. He figured Rutan would get a kick out of that.

He also told Rutan that he was driving to New Orleans as soon as he sent the email.

And he did. He got in his jeep right away, gassed up at a service station on the interstate, and was near New Orleans within an hour and a half. He called the broker and introduced himself as an agent for the FBI. The broker's name was Ted Bouche.

"Mr. Bouche, I understand you may have rented a place to the people we want to interview," Bishop told the broker and recited what Jenkins had told him.

"Sounds like my guys. The Police Chief said you'd be calling."

"I'd like for you to show me the place," Bishop said. "I'll be knocking on the door. If they're at home, I'll want the Police Chief to arrest them."

The broker said he'd be waiting for him in front of

the Monteleon in thirty minutes. That was how long Bishop told him it'd take to get there. He promised to notify the police to be ready.

Almost thirty minutes later, Bishop pulled up in front of the hotel. A man with dark hair and the consequences of too many two-martini lunches and good New Orleans' food showing around his stomach and on his fleshy face, was waiting.

He opened the door to Bishop's jeep and slid into the front seat. After introductory handshakes and names, he gave Bishop directions to the house. It was three blocks north of the Quarter's main business district.

Bishop stopped his jeep half a block away to look the place over. As reported, it looked to have been recently rehabbed.

Cars were parked in practically all spots on both sides of the street. Bishop had run into that before and had always parked in a garage when visiting the Quarter. Narrow streets and little or no parking. However, the broker said the house had a small parking garage at the rear Bishop could use for parking.

Bishop went down a small alley to the garage and pulled into the slot. He got out and went to the back door. The broker walked out of sight down the alley. He didn't want to be involved in the FBI's business and in particular didn't want any clients who had drifted into that side of the culture to think he'd "sold them out."

There was no doorbell, so Bishop knocked. No one answered, so he knocked again. Still no answer.

He walked around to the front and rang the doorbell.

When he got no answer, he stared into the front window.

Lights out. But looks vacant. Damn. Must have been tipped off. Son of a bitch! Moved out! Damn!

He called the broker who was still in back and asked him to come to the front. "Nobody's inside. Looks like they've moved out."

The broker was there within seconds.

"You speak the local language, the dialect, can you ask the neighbors what they know?"

He did. The neighbors told him that a U-Haul truck was in front of the house last night and two men were moving stuff into it. A third man was seen but wasn't doing anything.

Too old, Bishop thought.

"There's a U-Haul office not far from here," the broker told Bishop and gave him directions.

*****

Bishop flashed his FBI credentials at the desk clerk at the U-Haul office and asked for the address the men who'd rented the truck had given when they rented it. Where were they moving to?

The clerk didn't question Bishop's authority and immediately looked it up. The abuse of authority felt good to Bishop. He was usually on the receiving end.

"They said they were going to Mobile, Alabama. But didn't give an address, but they'll be turning in the truck at our Mobile office." She gave him the office address and phone number.

Bishop asked the broker for a copy of the check the men had used to rent the place. He guessed the account was already being closed but he'd give the info to the CIA. With their resources, they could find out sooner than he could.

Bishop thanked the broker and dropped him off at an office building on Canal Street. He parked in the building lot and called Rutan.

"Can you have somebody get to the Mobile U-Haul office in Mobile, Alabama, and see if they know anything about where the men who turned in the truck, I assume they turned it in, might have unloaded it." He also gave Rutan the corporate name used on the check and the account number and asked if he'd check the status of that account.

"I'm looking for the address given for the corporation," Bishop said. "I'm betting Janson will be closing that account and forming a new corporation for the new account right away. I assume it's Janson's corporation."

Rutan said he'd get on it right away.

"Son of a bitch," Bishop said out loud after he'd hung up. "Those guys are good. Somebody at the police department must have called and told them they'd better clear out before I showed up. I have to assume they'll also know we can trace the U-Haul to Mobile. And the corporate check."

Bishop drove to his cabin to wait. *I hope Rutan can get there first.*

Rutan didn't. By the time he had anybody get there, Janson – Bishop assumed – had apparently rented another truck from another company and kept moving. Likewise, he'd closed the corporate bank account and had the balance in the account sent to his attorney. The attorney wouldn't tell Rutan's man anything without a court order, which he got, but by the time he did, Janson had already picked up the check.

"No doubt he formed a new corporation and opened a new checking account for it. No way to track it down. And, who knows where they moved. They had to leave old man Terry someplace," Bishop told Rutan during a phone call.

"We're dealing with some smooth operators," Rutan said.

"I'd say. They've been around the block a few times. I'd guess Tyson has been giving Janson advice on that," Bishop said.

"Probably. He was a pretty good case officer before he retired."

"Too bad we don't have a crime we could charge him with. If we did, we could have police departments all over the country searching for him," Bishop said. "You feel comfortable dummying up a charge?"

"Not off the top of my head. I'll ask my boss what he thinks of the idea. It wouldn't look good for the agency to get caught doing something like that, but I'll let you know. Good idea. I just don't know if we'll want to do anything that shady."

He'd call back and say that they couldn't do it. Bishop cursed to himself and thought, *well, I'll see if I can come up with anything on my end. Guess I have to.*

Bishop brewed himself a cup of coffee and drank it with a croissant on the porch while he pondered. Unfortunately, nothing came to mind. He was mentally exhausted after all he'd been through the last couple of days, running into dead ends.

That night, he caught Kathy up on his frustrations.

She sympathized but had no better ideas for finding the guys than he'd come up with.

"So, what are you going to do?" she asked.

"Damned if I know. I may have to tell the DC bunch I'm retiring. Didn't do them any good and I don't have any other thoughts. I feel like I've shot my wad."

She laughed at his crude reply.

He told her he was going to sleep on it. In the past, he had done some of his best thinking at three o'clock in the mornings.

*****

Surely enough, at around three the next morning, he did have an idea. And as soon as Kathy had driven away after breakfast, he thought about it some more.

I was thinking that cousin Leon must have talked to Fred about how I was over there looking for them. That was why somebody shot at me. I was speculating but that was my thought. But, if he did tell Fred and if Fred tried and failed to shoot me, Fred might have decided to keep moving. I don't know if the timing works though. A better scenario might still be the police contact. Works better with the timing. Even so, my visit with Leon, assuming they talked, would have also put Fred on notice. And when Fred heard that the police were working with the real estate brokers to find them, again, assuming he had a police contact, he knew for sure he had to move on.

So, maybe I'd better pay Leon another visit. Put the fear of God into him this time. The chief's guys couldn't find him, but maybe I can. Or, maybe he's back at home by now.

*****

By ten that morning, he was parking on Leon's street half a block from the man's house. Bishop got out of his jeep and walked to the man's house. He thought that if Leon saw a car pull up, he'd exit out the back door. *That may be what he did when the chief's guys were in town.* An old pickup was parked in front of the house.

Looks like the same pickup that was here the last time I was in town, Bishop thought. Can't be two trucks that look that worn out. *So I'd say he's back.*

The chief's guys may have just accepted the truck as some kind of fixture. Goes with the house. Just about as old.

Bishop had a chuckle that he kept to himself.

He went to the door and knocked. He didn't see a doorbell. A television was on inside the house. He could see the screen through the front window.

Seconds later, Leon opened the door. When he saw Bishop, his face took on a frightened look and he started to close it but Bishop had already stepped inside.

"Too late, old buddy. Now, we're going to have a talk. I may have to arrest you. Drag your ass to Court. You may end up in a DC jail with some other smelly jail birds. You have broken the law! And you know what happens to people who break the Federal law! If you don't, you're sure as hell gonna find out!" He stared Leon in the eyes and added. "They end up in a Federal Pen, doing hard time."

Leon backed away. "I didn't do anything. I didn't. I swear to God!"

"You told Fred we were looking for him. We have proof."

Leon was shaking his head vigorously but was looking away like he was trying to come up with something to say.

"Can't lie your way out of it, Leon. Don't even try. We got you dead to rights." Bishop was bluffing but figured it would work with Leon.

"I jes tole him you'd come by here askin' 'bout him. He called. Whut could I do? He's my cousin. I'm sorry. I didn't go to break no law. He asked me whut you wanted. I tole him I'd heard them talking about New Orleans and I tole you that. That made him real mad."

"Well, you sure as hell broke the law and I have to

decide what to do with you," Bishop said. "Better sit your ass down. And this time I want some straight answers."

"I ain't got none to give you. I already tole you all I know," Leon said.

"I reckon you do. First of all, I want Fred's phone number."

Leon began shaking his head. "I ain't got it. He never gived it to me. I swear."

"Give me your phone," Bishop said.

Leon reached into his shirt pocket and handed the phone to Bishop.

Bishop noted that Leon and Fred had exchanged 2 phone calls. The second a day before. Bishop wrote down Fred's phone number that showed on the phone and said, "You called Fred twice. You –"

Leon interrupted and said, "I jes returned his calls. I didn't know his number."

"What'd he say?"

"He wus askin' me if anybody'd been by lookin' for 'im. I told him about your visit. How you threatened me."

"That was the first call. What about the second call?"

"Uh, he said they wus not in New Orleans any more."

No doubt about that.

"What else?" Bishop asked.

"Jes that he'd be in touch when they got settled. I ast 'im where they wus goin'."

"Where did he tell you?"

"Said he didn't know. Said they wus still lookin'."

"And you're going to call me when he tells you. Right?" Bishop asked. He knew damn well the man wasn't going to tell him anything.

"I shore am," Leon said.

"I'm not going to arrest you just now, Leon. Because you're going to tell me when Fred calls the next time. Aren't you?"

Leon was nodding his head up and down. His face bore a slight smile. "I thank you. I shore do. I'm much obliged to you."

I bet you are.

"Where else has Fred been talking about living? What towns?"

Leon began shaking his head again.

"You can stop with that bullshit, Leon. Just tell me where."

"I honestly don't rightly know, Mr. Bone. I shore don't. If I did, I'd tell you."

Sure you would.

"You know what's going to happen to you if I find out you lied to me?"

Leon shook his head but looked straight at Bishop. "Uh, whut?"

"A squad of police cars will surround this house and drag your sorry ass away. You'll spend the next ten years of your worthless life behind bars fending off hard-core lifers. Now, tell me!"

"Oh God. Oh God, I wish I knew. I do, Mr. Bone. I'd tell you," Leon said. "The onelyest place he ever talked about was New Orleans. Some place down there. Uh quarter or something. Someplace. I don't know. I didn't pay no attention. I knew I'd never go there. That's all I know, Mr. Bone, I swear to God."

Bishop figured he was telling the truth. He got into his jeep and headed to Lawton. It'd be time for Kathy by the time he got back. *Happy Hour.*

On the way to Lawton, he thought about what Leon had told him. Not a hell of a lot, but he'd think about it more during the night. Maybe something would come to him.

Kathy arrived within thirty minutes after he'd pulled in. He gave her a big hug and kiss. He was in the process of mixing the G&Ts they both loved. She had requested popcorn instead of the nuts they usually had. So he had the popcorn popping and with the salt he'd sprinkled on it, it tasted great.

As they enjoyed their happy hour, he told her about his day, and what he'd found out from Leon. "Not much," he said. "But something, I think, is lurking in my subconscious. I hope it's something useful.

"I do too."

She told him about her day. Not as exciting as his, but she always wanted to tell him. That way they stayed in touch with what the other one was doing.

He'd planned to barbeque hamburgers that evening. He'd left the meat out to thaw while he was in Alabama. So it was ready for the grill he'd fired up when he heard her drive up.

Thirty minutes after they'd finished their drinks, they

were putting the finishing touches on their hamburgers. Bishop also began fixing french fries using sweet potatoes. Kathy finished it up.

They enjoyed the dinner on the porch. The beavers worked until it was dark then they disappeared into their huts for whatever they did there.

"I wonder," Bishop said.

"Me to," Kathy replied. With a smile.

During the night, Bishop woke twice but didn't have the thought he was looking for. Leon had said something though that was hanging around in his mind.

What the hell is it? He asked himself but didn't get an answer.

The next morning though when Kathy was talking about her mother's life in Arizona, it came to him. Kathy was saying how much her mother loved living in Arizona even when she had the house in Lawton, she was still talking about Arizona. "She just loved the openness of it. It made her feel free," she had told Bishop.

"I think I understand. Sometimes a place gets to you," he'd replied.

Ah, a place like the French Quarter, he was thinking. *I figured Fred had moved out, but what if all that was just a dodge to make us think he was moving. Slick asshole. He might have gone back and did a deal with a private party, not a broker, to rent a place. He may still be down there.*

But how in the hell can I figure out where.

Ah, maybe I can. At least I can verify that he's still in

the French Quarter.

After Kathy had left for the library, he thought some more. "Who do I call to do it? Well, I'll start with the chief."

He called Chief Jenkins and explained what he'd thought, based on something Leon had said about Fred loving New Orleans.

"Good God, Bishop. A few more ideas like that and I'll be thinking you're ready for a train ride out of here. Did you tell Kathy? I bet if you did, she looked at you funny."

"I hear you Chief. Yeah, I may be ready for the bone yard, but do you have any better ideas. I bet you haven't found anything in Mobile."

He admitted that he had not, but that they were still searching. Bishop had gotten the same response from Rutan.

"Well, at least give my idea a try. I agree it's off the wall but I'm desperate. And desperate people come up with desperate ideas." He told him what he had in mind.

"You want to track Fred's telephone number and see where the phone is? Is that it?" He let out a loud sigh.

"Yes. I thought you might have somebody local doing that for your cases," Bishop said.

"I don't. We have done it occasionally, but when we do, we sub in out. Local company in Jackson does it for us. Not cheap. I have to write it up and get the mayor's office to approve it," the chief said. "He doesn't like spending money on speculative ideas like that."

"I see. Even though finding the location of the phone

might also locate the man who killed Watson, it – "

The chief finished the sentence for him. "It also might not help us find anything."

"Short sighted, Chief," Bishop said. "Now and then, you have to take a chance."

"Maybe so, but not with city money and somebody waiting to run against the mayor. For you, I'd try it. But I know the mayor would be asking me what I found out and how it was helping in the case."

"And you might not have shit to tell him," Bishop admitted.

"Fraid so, Bishop."

Bishop let out a loud breath of air. "Okay. I'll go to my back up. I just don't know the guys I'm working for well enough to ask, but since I have no choice I will. Let the devil take the hindmost," Bishop said.

"I'd say. It's their case. I don't see how they can say no." Jenkins said.

"I guess you're right. I just wanted to keep things quiet until I found something. The last excursion was a disaster. Everybody thought we had 'em and we didn't. It was embarrassing."

"I can imagine. As I said, I can try for you but I'd hate for both us to be party to a disaster."

Bishop told him it was okay. He'd ask his client for help. They could take it out of his fee if it didn't work.

"And, considering the luck I'm having, I'd be surprised if it did work. But since I don't have a choice, I'll do it."

The chief wished him good luck. "Let me know what

you find," he said as they ended the call.

So, first he sent Rutan a report of his interview with Leon. In the report, he asked for the same favor he'd asked the chief. He waited for a couple of hours before calling him.

*****

While Bishop was emailing Rutan, two men were leaving an Apple store near Jackson Square with a new iPhone.

"Hope that satisfies you," Fred Janson told the thin man with blond hair beside him. Fred was slightly overweight and a few years over sixty-five. He was almost six feet tall with a jowly face and firmly established smile rings that came from his profession as a salesman.

The man with him, Tyson Terry, was also sixty-five and an inch or so taller than Fred. His long, thin face showed a stoic demeanor as it had his entire career.

"Well, I told you they could trace your phone and find us. I used to do it."

"Hell, Tyson, they'd be looking in Mobile for us. They'd never think we'd be back in good time New Orleans," Fred said with a big smile.

"Well, after they'd found out we weren't in Mobile, they may figure we came back to New Orleans," Tyson said. "I would have."

"Well, I gave you that. That's why I got a new phone. You think your dad's okay?"

"He has a bed and he likes to sleep. I'd say he's okay. If he gets up, he can get a beer from the fridge."

"Good. Let's get a cup of coffee from the Café du Monde. By then, it'll almost be time to get some food someplace," Fred said.

"I'm glad we found a place we could rent. I didn't like the thing in the Garden District. Too formal to suit me. And I knew Dad wouldn't like the condo on Canal."

"I didn't disagree. I prefer the relaxed attitude of the Quarter too. I feel at home here," Fred said.

"Plus, we didn't have to involve a damn realtor and give that Bone bastard a way to track us."

"Good thinking to read the classifieds," Tyson said.

"Even so, I laid a few dollars on the guy at the Monteleon to keep a lookout for Bone. I'm glad Leon had the sense to get a photo of him on his phone. I gave the guy a copy."

"He could stay someplace else, but I'm betting that's where he'd stay if he comes down here looking."

"Well, if he does, I'll get a call and I'll be ready for the bastard. It pissed me off that somebody thinks he has the right to follow me around."

"Me too. I don't like people trying to control my life like that," Tyson said.

"Maybe they won't find us," Janson said.

"I'm not so sure. Couple of buddies I have left at the agency say it was the agency that hired Bone to find us. Word is he's damn good. Like a bulldog. Never gives up."

"Well, we just have to get him to change his

attitude," Janson said.

*****

Rutan answered Bishop's call. "Jerry," he said. "Bishop Bone calling I assume."

"I was wondering if you'd followed up on my suggestion to track Janson's phone."

"I have and I have results. First, I checked Mobile found nothing. So, as you suggested, I switched to New Orleans and found three addresses before I lost contact. I assume he got a new phone."

"I thought he might. Just glad you got three addresses. What are they?"

Jerry gave him the three. One was in the Garden District, another was just off Canal Street and another was in the Quarter a short walk from Bourbon Street.

"Plus, I had our guys run through the classified ads for rentals and found one close to the address I gave you. I called the number and found it had just been rented to three men, one elderly." He gave Bishop that address.

"Good thinking and good work," Bishop told him. "That's where I'll go tomorrow."

"Good luck."

Chapter 10

"If I can track Janson down in New Orleans, I still have to find him but I'll do that out of my fee," Bishop said to himself as he neared the Monteleon where he planned to stay that night. He'd walk to the address Jerry gave him the next morning.

He had the photos of both men in the inside pocket of the lightweight jacket he'd worn. It was pretty hot and humid weather but he'd also worn a short-sleeved shirt so he wasn't uncomfortable. He slid a small recorder into a pocket of his jacket. He could easily turn it on without reaching into the pocket.

"I want everything that's said recorded," Bishop told himself.

He had called Kathy and told her he had to hurry to New Orleans to catch Janson and Tyson before they could leave town again.

"Be careful, Bishop. You usually stir up trouble when you get into these situations," she said.

"I expect this time I'll be a sitting down, asking questions and leaving a meeting, nothing serious but I will watch my back," he said.

She said she might drive out to the cabin. "I love sitting on the back porch. It's better with you beside me, but I'll do the best I can," she said.

*****

Before he'd left Lawton, he'd asked the chief to alert Chief Allerman of New Orleans that he'd call if he found the three men at the address. He wasn't sure what they could be charged with but maybe they could be held on suspicion of something long enough for Bishop to question them if they balked at being questioned by him.

"Hell, I already have a note to do it," Jenkins said. "You'd better take something with you. You know what I mean. I wouldn't conceal a gun, might get caught with it."

"I'm a lawyer, Chief. I believe in the rule of law. It controls how people have to act if our culture is to continue to make progress. So far it has worked."

"I know about that, Bishop. I believe in the same thing, but now and then, when we're faced with death, we think survival ain't bad. That's what I'm talking about, survival. Now, getting back to reality, I don't know what the law is down there, but how about taking a piece of chain or a metal rod of some kind you can stick in your pocket in case things get rough. Hell, I may have something I could lend you. I'll tell Chief Allerman so he'll make sure his guys don't arrest you for carrying. If you decide to go that route."

"I don't know either man, but you might be right, especially if either or both killed Watson and tried to kill me. I'll see if I have anything in the pile of stuff I've picked up from helping you over the years. Could be

162

something I can use this trip to save my butt," Bishop said. "Thanks for your advice and your offer."

"I think you should call Chief Allerman when you get to town," Jenkins said.

"Hell, I would, but I don't have a thing more than suspicions to go on. I'm looking for something substantial."

"Well, good luck then."

What Bishop shoved into the pocket of the light jacket he decided to wear was a pair of brass knuckles he'd taken from a thug he and the chief had encountered in a case they'd handled. Bishop figured they'd be illegal in Louisiana but didn't figure he'd need them anyway. In any case, they shouldn't cause as much controversy as a revolver and firing off shots, if he had to use them and got caught, even if he was a friend of Chief Jenkins or was a fake FBI agent.

"I can throw the knuckles into the bushes assuming I'm still standing. No noise, not shell casings and nobody shot. Just blood all over. Hopefully not mine."

*****

He reached the French Quarter in the late afternoon and parked in the Monteleon's parking garage. He checked in to the hotel. As he did, he noticed a parking attendant pass and scrutinize him more carefully than he thought was necessary but he let it go.

Guy probably wonders why I'm dressed like I'm looking for a job, he thought.

Upstairs, he threw his overnight bag on the bed in his room and looked at his watch. It was a couple of minutes before five.

"Got here earlier than I'd figured. Hell, I can walk to their house and have my chat well before dark. I'll feel safer walking in the Quarter while it's daylight."

So he went downstairs and out the hotel's lobby door onto the street. The address was about a seven-block walk from the hotel. He figured he could make that in less than twenty minutes. As he left, he thought the parking attendant by the door again looked hard at him, even stared.

What the hell, Bishop thought, *maybe I am too informally dressed for the hotel. But, hell, this is the French Quarter. Informality is the order of the day.*

He didn't give it another thought, just hurried toward the address he'd been given by Rutan by the owner of the house Janson had rented.

As he walked, he noted that all parking spaces along the streets were still full. Driving slowly was the order of the day in the Quarter to avoid hitting parked cars and people walking across the street.

When he was about half way to the address, he noticed a blue compact pull onto the street behind him and stop as if the driver was waiting for someone to come out of one of the houses. So Bishop felt secure crossing the street. As he did, the car roared to a start and headed right at him. He managed to leap onto the hood of a parked car just in time to avoid being hit. As it was, the car's side mirror caught the heel of his shoe and knocked it a car length ahead.

The car never stopped.

"Damn, the son of a bitch was trying to kill me," Bishop said. "How in the hell did anybody know I was – . Ah, the hotel parking attendant. He must have been on the alert for me. Must have called Janson or Tyson. Damn. Well, whoever it was missed."

He put his shoe back on and hurried toward the house they had rented.

When he was about a block away, two men walked into the street ahead of him. One man was hitting the palm of his left hand with a blackjack and grinning. A blackjack was a leather pouch filled with lead balls used to hit people, usually men, over the heads when they didn't do as they were told, like Bishop was doing then.

Bishop walked down the center of the street. The sidewalks were so littered he preferred the street for walking.

The man with the blackjack called out, "You're gonna learn that some folks don't like nosey bastards following them around. Gonna hurt some," he laughed.

Bishop slipped his hand into his jacket pocket and felt a little more comfortable when his fingers slipped into the brass knuckles he'd brought. As he pulled his hand out, a noise he heard behind him caused him to look around. Behind him were two other men, both bearded and one also had a blackjack.

Well, looks like it's going to be a blood bath, mine.

He decided to make a run for it and turned to see if he could break through the guys at his back. He faked

165

like he was going to charge between them and they stepped closer together. He then twirled and hit the guy without the blackjack in the knee with his shoe. He heard a crack and he immediately swung his knuckles into the guys jaw. He went down like he'd been shot and wouldn't be fighting anymore that night.

But the other guy with a blackjack had swung at Bishop's head while Bishop was disabling his companion. Bishop ducked as best he could, but the blackjack grazed his forehead and cut it. Bishop could feel the blood coming down the side of his head.

He ducked again to avoid the guy's next swing and as soon as he had, he came up and caught the guy in the ribs with his brass knuckles. He heard a loud crack and the guy fell back against a parked car moaning and holding his ribs. He too was out for the night.

By then, the two guys who'd been facing Bishop in the street, were all over him with lefts and rights. They also wore big rings on both hands and when they hit, they drew blood. Bishop got in his licks as well, but they were hitting him more that he was hitting them. He ducked to avoid some punishment but not enough. He felt the blackjack thud against his back. Their fists were smashing him in the face. He backed away to avoid some punishment, ducked and charged into the guy with the blackjack, knocking him back a step. As he did, Bishop hit the guy in the face with his brass hardware, knocking out most of his front teeth. He followed that with a left into the guy's stomach, sending him dazed to his knees, his mouth open.

His buddy swung at Bishop but Bishop stepped away and his fist missed. Bishop swung his knuckles at the man who moved to one side to avoid the brunt of it. Even so, it caught the guy's arm. Bishop heard another crack.

The man stepped back and glanced around. He was the only one of the four still standing. He didn't like the odds of fighting a man with knuckles by himself. Hearing the distant sound of police sirens headed their way, he turned and ran.

Bishop heard the sirens also. "Damn," he mumbled. "I'd better get out of here too."

He didn't want to be answering questions that might embarrass or put Chief Allerman in a conflict situation, so he took off too, heading down the first alley he saw and then on a street that would take him to the hotel. He was a block away before the two police cars reached the scene of the brawl. All the police would find were pieces of teeth the one man had lost and some blood, most of which was Bishop's but some belonged to the guys he had hit with his knuckles.

Bishop went into the hotel through the parking garage. He was careful to avoid the attendants and was equally careful going up the stairs to the floor where his room was located.

He went inside and patched himself up as best he could from the first aid kid he kept in his overnight bag, a necessity for the work he often did. He looked in the mirror and figured he might be arrested if he showed himself in public. So he called the desk, and paid his bill by phone and checked out.

He made his way down the stairs to his car in the garage and drove to his cabin. He was home by ten and exhausted.

He was initially surprised to see Kathy's car but then remembered she'd said she might come out. He was glad.

She's gonna be upset, he thought as he rode the elevator up.

And she was. "What happened to you?! You fall into a meat grinder?"

"No, fell into a disagreement with four men. They didn't care for the odds and set about to even them up. They lost." He told her he'd give her the full story after he'd taken a bath to get cleaned up.

He took a shower to wash off any blood he'd missed at the hotel. Afterward, Kathy took care of his cuts and bruises, mostly the cuts. The bruises would have to heal by themselves.

As she worked, he told her what had happened.

"Four men and you survived? I'm surprised to see you."

He told her about his brass knuckles and how they'd probably saved him from a serious beating.

He thanked her for her medical patchwork.

"You needed it," she said. "A couple could use a stitch or two but I guess you'll heal up with a few more scars to go with the ones you already have."

"Comes with the territory," he said.

"You need to move to another territory," she quipped.

He laughed.

She poured wine for both while Bishop emailed Jerry Rutan a report with a blind copy to the chief. Tired as he was, and as beaten up, doing that report took some effort, but he knew it needed to be done. It was almost eleven by the time he'd finished.

After he'd sent the report out, he sat in his back-porch rocker with the creek lights on and enjoyed the wine with Kathy.

His phone rang. It was Chief Jenkins. "At it again, huh?" he said.

"I guess."

"Must have taken something along to give you some help if you backed off four thugs. Sounds like that's what they were," he said.

"My guess too. I figure Janson or Tyson hired them along with the guy in the car, to make sure I didn't get to their house to see them. One of the guys, one with a blackjack, said something about nosey people following others around. I figured from that comment that they were planning to teach me a lesson. From the looks of me, I guess they did."

"But you were the last one standing. Damn, Bishop, you're either one tough son of a gun or lucky as hell," the chief said.

"I'd say lucky. One of those blackjack hits and I'd have been on the street getting the shit kicked out of me," Bishop said.

"I sent a copy of your report to Chief Allerman. He'll probably call you in the morning. I figure he'll know you were the central figure in the fracas," he said.

"I'll fill him in. I would have stayed but hell, I didn't feel like spending an hour explaining what happened after I threw away my knuckle hardware," Bishop said.

"Yeah. Probably just as well. Anyway, you can explain it in the morning," Jenkins said. "I'm glad you got through it."

"I will. Thanks for calling." Bishop hung up. He had to sleep on his back all night, a big sacrifice because he enjoyed being close to Kathy in bed. He was afraid if he slept on his side, one of his cuts would open up and ruin the sheets.

Kathy did the breakfast honors with oatmeal, not one of Bishop's favorites, but he went with the flow especially since he didn't have to fix it.

Soon after she'd left for the library, he received the call from Chief Allerman.

"Bishop Bone," the man said in a deep growly voice that carried with it a tone of confidence. "Is that you?"

"It is. And you must be Chief Allerman. Chief Jenkins said you'd be calling. What can I do for you?"

"I got a copy of your report. Hell of a note. One man, fighting off four men in the middle of the Quarter. I've read some of your doings over the years working with Chief Jenkins. I guess they weren't overstating your qualifications one bit."

"I don't know. Now and then I get lucky. I got lucky last night. Your police sirens scared them off. When they heard you coming, they hauled ass."

"Neighbors say 'the big 'un in the middle' had done

170

knocked them others down, except for one. And, when he was the last one standing to face you, he ran like hell. The others slipped away too. You should've called me I'd 'a sent a couple of guys with you."

"Yeah. I thought about it, but frankly, I don't have a damn bit of evidence I could get past the worst lawyer in town. All I have are motives and suspicions. That's why I was there, to see if I could get anything that'd stand an objection in court."

"Hell, Bone, down here we're kind of friendly; if I tell the DA I think somebody's guilty, he believes me and will issue me a warrant. If I make a mistake, which I do now and again, we have a beer and a laugh together."

"I'll remember that next time. I didn't want to put you in an embarrassing position."

"I don't get embarrassed. I wait till my face loses the red and I sit down to figure out how to get even. So, how can I help you? I assume you're okay? From what the neighbors told us you took some shots."

"I did. I look like something out of a Hollywood movie, all bandaged up. But, if you're asking and if you don't mind sticking your neck out, I'll tell you."

"Let's hear it," he said.

"Well, I don't think I want to walk down that street again. I might not get lucky next time. What I'd like for you to do, if you don't mind making a fool of yourself, like I do now and then, is arrest Fred Janson and Tyson Terry. There's an old man with them, he's Tyson's father. Harmless. Tyson takes care of him. Apparently always has. You can leave him."

"Okay, I arrest the two of them. What then? I don't know beans about the case you're investigating for the … FBI … Jenkins told me a little about it."

"Well, after you get them in cells, I'd like for you to call me. I can be there in a couple of hours. I want to grill them. I can also brief your DA if he wants to join in. The FBI would appreciate all the help it can get."

Chief Allerman laughed. "I bet. Well, send me all you can. I'll discuss it with the DA. Hell, we may join in with you. We like hunting down the bad guys."

Bishop promised to get him a full report within the next two hours and did. He suggested to Chief Allerman they should search the house for a 410 gauge shotgun and shells and a Glock automatic with cartridges.

In the report, he'd said, "Fletcher Watson was killed with the shotgun and I somebody with a Glock attempted to kill me as well."

Allerman called him after he'd read it. "Damned if you ain't got yourself a real can of worms, Bishop Bone. You grab one and another one wiggles. Well, I'm gonna send a man out there to keep a look out on the house. I'll arrest them … probably tomorrow unless I see something that says I can drag 'em in now."

"I thank you Chief. I'll be waiting for your call."

"I'd say you'll be hearing from me tomorrow. It'll take that long for the DA to get me the warrants I need, search and arrest warrants."

"That's a big assed relief, Chief. I wouldn't look forward to having to walk that route again from the hotel to the house. They may not miss next time."

"They be the ones relieved, if I believe what one lady told us. You were knocking 'em down."

Bishop laughed and hung up.

He spent the day calling his bank clients mostly to check in but also to say hello. He didn't want anybody to forget him. *Money doesn't grow on trees even if I have more than one of every kind of trees that grows in this part of the country.*

Nobody had any business for him. Loans were current and none were even in the "sometimes late" category. There were some inspections, but they were so minor, the banks were handling them internally.

Bishop thanked them all.

The chief came out in the afternoon, ostensibly for a beer, but Bishop knew mostly he wanted to see what he looked like after having a brawl with four tough guys.

When Bishop heard the car drive up, he checked the window and when he saw it was the chief, he had a couple bottles of beer and glasses on the porch table waiting when the chief walked up.

He stopped and stared at Bishop. "Damn. Somebody's gotta teach you how to duck, Bishop. I'd hate to see what the other side looks like if you look like you do. Most likely have to wear sun glasses to look at 'em."

"I didn't take the time to inspect them, frankly. When we heard the police cars coming to my rescue, my assessment, we all hauled ass. I will say that three of them weren't running. They were dragging legs and holding ribs. Most likely, like me, they were wiping some blood out of their eyes."

"You do get yourself into some hostilities, Bishop. Ever heard about peace? Talkin' is lots easier than fightin'. Leaves more time for a cold beer."

Bishop grunted his approval.

Jenkins and Bishop talked about the fight he had for the rest of their beer and the one that followed. When they'd had their two, the chief got up to leave.

"Chief Allerman called and said he'd talked to you. He's gonna help you out. Maybe you won't have to work for the … FBI much longer. Kind of hazardous to your health."

"Can't say it'd bother me if they let me go," Bishop said. "I kind of like my bank jobs. I don't end up looking like a Hollywood mummy at the end of a day."

The chief looked at him a last time, shaking his head in wonderment as he did. "You sure as hell do. I bet that one guy might be willing to let you do some snooping next time he sees you." Bishop had mentioned the guy's quip in his report.

"I hope so."

*****

The next day Allerman called Bishop. "Got some news. Not particularly good, but it is news. The old man Mr. Terry died. We were set to serve the warrant when we found out. So, they're going to have a funeral and a burial for him. Gonna take a few days. My guess is it'll be next week before we can get in there."

"Yeah. I'd guess that's about right," Bishop said. "Have to let 'em have their hour of grief. What'd he die of?"

"Heart attack, I'm told," Allerman said.

"No doubt. He looked ready for one when I saw him."

"I'll call you when I know the old man's been buried."

Bishop hung up and sent Rutan and the chief a report of the latest development. "One damned frustration after another," was the way he ended it.

Both said they understood. They had had a few themselves.

Chapter 11

The following week, Allerman called to say they were serving the warrant that morning and arresting both men. And, then they were going to search the old house inside and out.

He said the men were still there. Bishop figured they must have assumed he was scared away or maybe they were just distracted by the old man's death. *At any rate, I'm glad they're still around.*

When Allerman showed up with the warrant and searched the house, both men objected and called their attorneys. Nevertheless, they were carted off to the New Orleans jail while the house was being turned upside down searching for a shotgun and a Glock.

"Didn't find either," Allerman said when he called Bishop.

"Damn, I'd hoped you would. Maybe they threw them away." But he knew that was wishful thinking. They didn't throw them away. Logically, they just didn't have a shotgun or a Glock.

Probably barking up another wrong tree, he thought. *If they had 'em, they'd probably have kept them, thinking nobody was ever going to catch up with them,* Bishop thought. *Case is still open.*

"Okay," he asked Allerman, "when can I question them?"

"Anytime you want, but they have attorneys. And they know how to go to court and get orders to have their clients released. So, if I were you, I'd get down here as soon as possible."

It was almost noon then.

"I'll be there by two," Bishop said. He was putting on decent looking clothes as he was punching off to end the call.

And he was parking in front of the jail house at a quarter till two. Allerman wasn't around, but he'd see him before he left town.

He'd decided to interview Tyson first and was shown to his cell by one of the jailers.

Tyson stood when Bishop entered. He looked remarkably healthy, tall, lean; not handsome, but his face showed a sense of dedication. He offered his hand which Bishop took. *Wants to be friendly,* Bishop thought. *Bastard wants to throw me off the scent, I guess. Maybe why they didn't move out when they knew we were on to them. Well, that didn't work.*

A table had been placed in the room with two chairs. Bishop took one and Tyson took the other. He set his recorder on the table in front of him.

"You mind?" he asked.

Tyson shook his head to indicate he didn't. Bishop noted it for the recorder.

As he had been doing with Julia, Bishop opened the questioning with a bluff. "Mr. Terry, we have witnesses that place you on Fletcher Watson's driveway the day he was murdered. That's one reason you were arrested and will be charged with murder. Did you kill him for revenge because you blamed him for forcing you out of the agency? Because of his false claim that you were selling secrets to the Russians or some foreign country?"

Tyson had stood and stepped back as soon as Bishop had begun talking but he'd not interrupted.

"I don't know any witness that could be. I was at Watson's place once to have it out with him. He framed … well, tried to frame me for something I didn't do. I think he did it to make sure he'd have no competition for Julia, but mostly because I did a hellofa better job with cases than he could ever imagine. He was slow and, in my opinion, lazy. Maybe that was because he was … hell, I'll say it, a bit on the stupid side. Took him twice as long to finish a case than it did me. He got tired of me getting all the accolades and tried to frame me. I told him that when I went to his house."

"The witness saw you the day he was shot," Bishop said with a straight face, staring him in the eyes.

"If the witness says that, you should give them a detector test. They have to be lying. I was taking care of my dad in Coffeeville when Watson was shot. He's had a slight, had, hell, he's dead now. Anyway, he had a slight stroke and I was seeing after him. I'd hired a woman to come in and help. She needed a break and I was giving her one."

He asked for Bishop's pen and wrote down the woman's name and phone number. "Call her. She'll tell you. I was there before dad's stroke and stayed for a few days, I don't remember how many, until he was up and about."

"The witness also says she – it was a woman – saw

your white compact parked on the road near where somebody tried to kill me with a Glock." He added a date and time.

Tyson laughed. "White compact? How many white compacts must there be in this world. Do you think anybody would charge me with murder based on owning a white compact. I wasn't there and I didn't shoot at you. If I had, you'd be dead." He took his iPhone out of his pocket and pushed the apps around, apparently checking something, After a minute, he looked up and said. "I was in New York that day with Fred, the man I live with – I'm sure you know that I'm gay. I was trying to get Julia to pretend to be my wife – she's a lesbian, I'm sure you know. Anyway, Fletcher didn't like it because he's annually retentive, and thinks what he wants is his. An unevolved creatine."

Bishop nodded. *Lesbian, be damned. That's a surprise. Maybe I did see a strange car coming away from her house.*

"Fred had asked me to help him make a presentation to the executives of a company interested in a security system he was selling. They bought it."

He gave Bishop the name of that company and their phone number.

"I don't remember the names but somebody in the company will remember that I was there."

Bishop turned off his recorder. He was certain Tyson wasn't his man.

"I imagine the agency will send somebody down here to question you," Bishop said. "They're still trying to track down the leak."

Tyson grimaced. "Hell, I don't know, but I've got nothing better to do right now. Lawyer's trying to get us out. I guess you're stalling that. They'll probably send Rutan down here to kick me around. He's usually their guy for that. They like to kick you when you're down. I think their theory is, anything said while you're hurting or in pain is always the truth."

He went on to say that he was never in favor of hurting anybody. Fred had a thing about people checking on him. He treasured his privacy. Bishop inferred from what he was saying that Fred was the one who hired the attacks on Bishop. He didn't say that exactly however.

Well, I've heard that gay people love as intensely as straights. If somebody insulted Kathy, I'd be upset enough to do something. I guess what I'd do would depend on the insult. Not my problem. Somebody killed Fletcher and shot at me. Those are my problems. Could be that neither Tyson nor Janson did either personally, but they could have had one of their goons to it. Well, Janson would be my choice for the jobs. Fletcher tried to frame Tyson. That might very well have pissed Janson off enough to send his goons to take revenge.

Bishop stood. "Good luck to you," he said as he left Tyson sitting in his chair.

In the hall outside, he thought, *another dead end. Nothing but dead ends in this case. Damn, I'd like for once to pull a string with something at the other end. Gotta tell Rutan. He may want to come down here and interrogate the man.*

As soon as he was finished with his interviews and was home, he'd call Rutan and tell him all Tyson had said. And he'd send a report with a transcription of his recordings to him with it.

As Tyson had assumed, Rutan would be on the next plane to New Orleans to talk to him. But he'd find out nothing useful and tell Bishop that the sale of another CIA secret had turned up. It was not all that important, but it had come from their files.

Bishop got about the same results from Janson that he'd gotten from Tyson. He told him that the authorities had witnesses that placed somebody who looked like him near Watson's place the day he was shot.

Janson laughed at the bluff. He was in the east making his rounds, and gave Bishop names and numbers to call.

"Pretty good alibis for a man responsible for trying to kill me the other evening," Bishop said.

"Not me, asshole. However, I've heard that some people just damn well don't like assholes following them around, snooping into their business. You might want to keep that in mind as you go through life, whatever's left of it anyway. I didn't do any of the shit you're going on about. So go bother somebody else."

"Chief Allerman's going to arrest the four men and the driver of the car who tried to kill me. And guess who's going to jail? You, asshole. Get ready for prison and the tough-as-nail lifers who still have animal instincts they want satisfied."

"Get out!"

Bishop picked up his recorder and did just that.

*****

Chief Allerman had been waiting in his office to see him after his interviews. He got up and shoved out his hand when Bishop poked his head in.

Allerman was a big, rawboned man. He had a big, rough face with deep age lines, big hands and long arms. From his telephone calls, Bishop had already assessed his voice as having originated from the remotest region of hell.

"Pleasure to meet you, Bishop Bone. Oddly enough, I've read things about you from time to time, helping my ole buddy Chief Jenkins solve cases."

"The chief has saved my ass a number of times. I can tell you that. He's a good man," Bishop replied.

"I know. I can always depend on him doing what he says he's gonna do."

"Pardon me for asking, but did you ever box? I'd bet you'd be a hard man to hit, and harder to bring down," Bishop said with a smile.

Allerman laughed. "Be damned. Not many people know it but when I was at LSU, we won the national boxing championship. I was the heavyweight. Knocked out everybody they sent after me."

Bishop congratulated him. "You look the part, Chief. You must have had two inches reach on anybody you faced. Tough to hit, I figure."

"You're not the first to say that. Thanks though. So, what'd you find out?"

Bishop gave him his conclusions and his frustrations about finding nothing.

"Best I can figure, Janson decided to take revenge for Watson's claim that Tyson was a traitor."

"Yeah. I understand what you're saying."

"No way in hell to prove it though, unless you can find the four goons who tried to teach me a lesson for snooping – also Janson's doings, no doubt. Unless you can find them, or the guy in the car who tried to run me down, and get them to talk, you might as well turn both of them loose and close the case. But maybe hold them for a couple more days to see if somebody else from the … FBI wants a crack at them. I'll be sending them my report later today. Oh, that reminds me. From what I could see, the driver of the car was a younger man. He had a Louisiana tag." Bishop gave him what he thought were the first two digits of the tag.

Allerman said he'd check it out. "If I find anybody, I'll drag 'em in and sweat the truth out of them. I'm checking hospitals and medical facilities for anybody coming in to be patched up and wrapped up. I'll find one of them! You can count on it. I think I have a pretty good idea about who was involved. Let you know when I find out for sure."

Bishop thanked him and shook his hand. "Damn, Chief. I bet you're still a pretty tough man in a fight."

Allerman laughed. "Maybe so Bishop Bone, but you're not bad yourself. I'd be honored and feel completely secure standing back to back with you in any brawl."

Bishop laughed.

Bishop drove home and even though he wanted a fresh cup of coffee, he wanted to finish his work by getting his reports to Rutan and Chief Jenkins. He knew that both were waiting. When he was tired and wanted to quit for the day, he reminded himself of something an old man he worked for on a construction crew had said when some of the others wanted to quit early. He'd said, "A job half done, ain't no job at all." That quip had become Bishop's mantra over the years. When he wanted to quit, he remembered what the man had said and kept working until the job was done.

And so he did. He sent both men a report of what he'd done in New Orleans, what he'd learned. Not much. He also mentioned the recordings if they wanted transcripts. He closed with the comment that he didn't think either man had done the shootings personally, but that Janson probably had connections with people who would for a fee. And, he had a motive. "His lover had been wronged by Watson and I was trying to find who did it. So I had to go."

Rutan called, as Bone had anticipated, and said he would be flying to New Orleans on the next flight. He'd send Bishop a report of anything relevant he learned.

Bishop went to the kitchen to brew a cup of coffee. He would also warm a croissant and enjoy them on the porch. As he took his first sip of coffee, Chief Jenkins called.

"Just read your report. Still striking out, Bishop. Knowing you, I doubt that sits well with you."

"You're right. I'm on the back porch wondering what else I can do. I'm having to wait for Chief Allerman to arrest the goons who tried to bash my head in. He thinks they'll point the finger at Janson," Bishop said. "And he'll let us squeeze Janson for Watson's murder … and my shooting."

"And you think Janson will start talking to save himself some exposure to the death penalty."

"I'm hoping. But Janson's pretty savvy, a tough old bird. I don't know how much we can get out of him, but that's the slim reed I'm hanging onto right now. I'm hoping the cup of coffee I'm drinking will stimulate my brain some."

"You need a beer. I'll be out this afternoon. Give you a lift."

"Come on out. Beer's in the fridge, cooling," Bishop said.

*****

About four, the chief came up the stairs. Bishop already had a couple beers opened.

"You're late, I've already started," Bishop said.

The chief took his. "Better catch up then."

They mostly hashed what Bishop had already told him in his report and over the phone but he'd left out what Tyson had told him about Julia.

"One thing I didn't put in the report, and I don't

185

attach any relevance to it, but Tyson told me Julia is lesbian."

The chief looked shocked. "Son of a gun. Who'd have guessed that? We have a few gays and lesbians in town. Nobody much gives a damn so long as they keep it quiet."

"I've never met one."

"Most keep their private lives private," the chief said.

"That's the only surprising thing that came out of my drive to New Orleans."

"Should 'a got yourself a cup of coffee while you were in town," the chief said with a chuckle.

Bishop agreed.

"Well, where are you going next, Mr. FBI agent?"

"I wish to hell I knew. I don't have a clue. I'm hoping Chief Allerman will find one of the thugs I crossed swords with and squeeze a confession out of one. Have you found anything else out? Purvis and his sick stomach?"

"Somebody who was walking her dog heard we were asking questions about him. She called to say she'd seen him drive in. He was getting out of his truck before the garage door closed. Bent over, she said."

"Well, I guess we can cross him off the list. You find any other pissed off husbands?" Bishop asked.

He said nobody had come forward, but he hadn't been working the case. "It's basically Big Jim's case. I helped out in the beginning, but once you took over I sat and watched," Jenkins said.

"Best way to do it. I'm going to catch up with my

186

yard work and wait until some bank work comes in. I'll probably resign from the … FBI. I'm not doing them any good."

"Tilting at windmills, looks like."

"My thought as well. When the man I report to finishes what he's doing, I'll likely tender my resignation. I found Tyson and I've concluded that he didn't kill anybody. I think I can say I did what they were paying me to do."

"But knowing you, you still have the bit between your teeth," the chief said with a smile.

"I guess you know me better than most, Chief. Until somebody is convicted or confesses, it'll likely stay in my mind," Bishop said.

"Yep. Well, I gotta get home. June's expecting me to take her to dinner. She's celebrating something. I'll remember hopefully."

"Have a good one," Bishop said. "Kathy's probably on her way. We'll have G&Ts and catch up on each other's news. Maybe I'll invite her to eat out. That might take the edge off my failure."

"Good idea."

With that, the chief got up and went home.

By the time Bishop had the drinks mixed, Kathy was coming up the stairs. And before they'd finished, she'd agreed that a steak dinner would be great.

They went to their usual place in the country where the steaks were organic.

His side of the conversation during dinner was a repeat for the most part of what he and the chief had discussed. She was surprised to learn Julia's preference but not shocked.

"Lawton has its share. I know several. Nobody can help being born the way they are. They probably wake up and recognize that their sexual preferences are different. In our culture they also recognize that it's best to keep it a secret since the majority of the people are …. straight, I guess people say."

"I guess. I don't think it makes a difference to the case," he said.

She shook her head. "I was just wondering. Good steak."

*****

Bishop spent the next day working outside. Nobody shot at him but he kept an eye open while he pruned, weeded, and cut the grass. Around noon he quit working then went inside and had a shower. After that, he rewarded himself with a coffee and croissant on the porch. He let his thoughts wander, hoping they'd wander someplace useful. They didn't but his phone rang.

"Mr. Bone," Rutan said when Bishop answered. "I'm at the airport getting ready to fly back to DC. Tyson absolutely denied selling anything to anybody. But Chief Allerman found the four guys who tried to beat you up, kill you, I'd guess. They've been charged. They said Tyson paid them to do it. They also gave him the name of the guy who tried to run you down. After I confronted Tyson with that information, he got cooperative."

"I'm glad to hear that. I hope they get some time in a maximum security prison."

"Allerman said they would but they'll get some time off for cooperating."

"Yeah," Bishop said, agreeing.

"Anyway, Tyson gave me a bank account number and told me I could check. He wrote me an authorization for the bank to give me all of his transactions since he'd retired."

"I wonder why he'd had such secrecy? Seems like he had something to hide," Bishop said.

"My conclusion as well, and that's what I told him. He said it wasn't him. He said his partner, Fred, had an absolute thing about privacy. Psychological, he called it. Fred apparently didn't want anybody knowing anything about what he was doing and why. Tyson said he just went along."

"I can understand Tyson's thinking. Why have a fight with your significant other over nothing much?"

"I guess. But we still have the leak to find. We're definitely sure that something was sold after they'd all retired. I agree with you, neither man shot Watson. I'm not saying Janson didn't hire it done, as you say, but they didn't do it personally themselves."

"I'm hoping the New Orleans police can find something that implicates Janson," Bishop said. "But, Jerry, I'm out of things I can do. I'll give it a few days. Maybe something will come up, but as of now, I'm out of ideas."

"I hear you. We are too. We're going to have to rethink our stagey. See if we can come up with a new approach. I'll be doing that when I get back to DC. If you come up with anything, let me know. We've been pleased with all you done. I know you haven't solved our problem or found the killer, but you found Tyson. That was big as far as we were concerned. Good job. We'll talk again, down the road."

I guess I told him as much as I need to. I more or less said I was going to resign. I'll give it a few days before I make it official.

They ended their conversation.

Lacking nothing better to do, Bishop got out his guitar and sang some old country western songs as off key as the chords he plucked.

Soon Kathy came home and they enjoyed a fun evening together.

And, that night at three, nothing woke him up, telling him where he could go next in search of answers. So he got a good night's sleep instead.

The next morning they had coffee and toast on the porch with a rasher of bacon to give it some zip.

"Kathy, I love you," Bishop said. "I know I get busy now and then and don't tell you, but you're my raison d'être."

She reached over and put her hand over his with a big smile. Then she leaned over and gave him a big kiss. "And, Mr. Bone, you're mine. My life begins when I come up the steps and find you here."

Chapter 12

Some buddies from the Lawton Country club called the next day and asked if he'd play tennis with them that morning. He agreed. They usually managed to play once or twice a week when four became available. That morning, they split two sets and had lunch at the Country Club. He caught up on the local gossip.

The mayor of twelve years had announced his retirement, so the rush was on by half a dozen others to take his place. One of the guys at the table laughed and said, "I heard his wife made him retire or she was going to tell the world 'about his thing with the maid.' I don't know if that's true, but she said she wanted some time with him before they went to that place the preachers talk about."

Bishop told himself to ask the chief about the rumor, especially the one about the maid. Juicy bit of gossip.

Nothing better to do than look for gossip. I must be losing it.

They parted company, promising to get together the next week for another round, and Bishop headed for the locker room.

Coming out of the shower, his phone rang. It was a bank client. *A case?* Bishop thought hopefully.

"Bishop," the man said, "Gotta problem we need for you to look into. Are you free?"

"I think so," Bishop said. *Praise the lord. A problem. Thought I was going to be doing yard work the rest of my days.*

The bank client, whose name was Larry Ashley, explained the problem. The bank approved a five million dollar construction loan for a strip center in a relatively small town in central Mississippi. The borrower got half through the project and suddenly just wrapped it up and moved to another small town thirty miles away to begin another strip center identical to the one he'd just finished. When the bank heard about it, they stopped funding the loan and asked the borrower to propose an amendment to do what he was doing.

The borrower, Wesley Adams, more or less told them to kiss his ass. "You approved the loan. I'm not asking for more. I just decided to put half the center in one town and the other half in another town."

"But, that's not what the bank approved. And what was approved had the support of a marketing study. That study said the town you're in would support the center we approved. We know nothing about the marketing support of a center in the other town. We don't want you to get the thing built and nobody shows up to buy anything. Or, come to that, you can't get tenants."

Their arguments went back and forth for a number of weeks. The bank stopped disbursements and called in the loan. The borrower didn't any tenants for the new center but had prospects. However, even fully leased, the income wouldn't support the loan. So, the bank had a loan in default and a borrower who was determined not to comply with the loan conditions as approved.

"So, we are calling you. We might very well approve an amendment to the loan, but the borrower has to provide a new application supported by a marketing study that includes both centers. In fact, the president of the bank wants the borrower and somebody from the marketing company to appear at the bank to answer questions about the project. We don't want the borrower to put a little extra in the marketing company's sock to say what he wants it to say."

"In effect, the loan committee wants to eyeball the borrower and the marketing company to see if they are being totally up front with the bank."

"The borrower has already decided to amend the loan program without our approval. We don't trust him anymore. Can you go see him and bring him in?"

"Give me his address and I'll go up there tomorrow and have a visit with the guy," Bishop said. He also asked for the address of the other site he wanted to build the second strip center on. *Need to look at it in case anybody asks me for a marketing opinion. I'm not totally qualified but I can give an opinion.*

"I'll warn you the guy has a temper," Larry said. "He thinks what he says is the gospel and anybody who disagrees would be better off dead. That's the attitude I see when I've dealt with him."

"Sounds like a tough guy," Bishop said.

"I think he is. We relied heavily on the marketing study when we made the loan. That study only covered the one strip center the guy now wants to rent as is."

"I'll anticipate a rough reaction," Bishop said.

Ashley gave Bishop the man's name and address and emailed him a copy of the loan approval. Bishop thanked him and promised a report by the end of the next day.

Kathy was happy for Bishop. She knew he became lethargic if he was without something to do for too long or was unable to solve a problem he'd been given.

*****

Bishop decided to look at the second site first. *See what the guy's done. Hell, he may be well into building it. The bank needs to know.*

He pulled up alongside the site. A bulldozer was moving a pile of debris and dirt from the center of the vacant lot. It was in the commercial part of the small town.

Probably a decent site for something commercial. I don't know if the town will support a strip center though.

The driver of the bulldozer stopped to drink from a bottle next to him. Bishop took the opportunity to ask him a couple of questions.

"Looks like somebody's gonna be building. What's it going to be, a strip center?" he asked.

The man looked at him as if assessing whether or not he was asking anything he could answer. Finally he said, "About to start a strip center. Town needs one. People having to drive thirty miles to get what they need."

"Owner has a loan I guess?" Bishop asked.

Again, the man scrutinized Bishop a second or two before answering. "Yeah. Loan's been approved. Money's waiting."

Money may be waiting, just not for this address. Another thought zipped through Bishop's mind but it was too quick for him to catch it. *If it's important, it'll come back,* he told himself.

"Good luck to you," he told the guy on the dozer and left.

He drove to the town where the other center was supposed to be built with the loan. He parked on the street. The small center was finished. Signs were already up announcing shops for lease. A muscular man, Bishop assumed to be the owner, talked with a couple of guys in what Bishop assumed would be the parking lot. All were wearing work clothes. The man with the muscles looked tough like the loan manager had said.

Saved the paving until last so it wouldn't get messed up during the construction, Bishop thought.

The men finished their meeting. The muscular man headed back to a small construction trailer at the back of the lot. The others got into a truck and drove away.

Bishop followed the man into the trailer.

When the man saw Bishop, he turned and asked, rapid fire, "What do you want? Who are you? You from the bank?"

"Right to the point then?" Bishop said and told him who he was and why he was there.

"Haven't seen you before. Another guy did a couple of inspections."

"I get involved when a loan is in default," Bishop said. "You're Wesley Adams, I assume."

"Default? What the hell are you talking about? I haven't even finished. I'm not supposed to make any payments for a couple more months. Need time to get the center leased up. Already got two. And, a couple more are interested. So, what's the shit about default? Larry's been bitching about me building on two sites. Half here and half in a little town down the road. I can pay on the loan I used to build this center from my leases here."

"Maybe so, but I think that's the problem, Mr. Adams. The loan was approved for this site and the marketing study you presented for it only dealt with this site and the center covered by the plans. What you're proposing is using half the loan to build on another site. That was not part of the loan committee's approval, and in effect is an anticipatory breach of the loan agreement you signed."

"So what? Hell, money is money. Why in hell do they care where the money comes from to repay the loan? Lots of people wanted a small center over yonder so I made the decision to build half a center here and half there. When things get up and going, I'll build the other half here. Plenty of room." He waved at the lot. Gotta put in the parking lot and it's ready to open. Few days. I was just talking to them."

"The bank has regulators who look over their shoulders. They would take exception if the bank allowed you to decide how the loan proceeds were spent.

Right now, you told the bank you were going to build a larger center here. And the marketing study said it should lease up within three months. Lease payments from the tenants would more than cover the entire loan balance. By dividing up the loan, you won't have enough income to cover the entire loan when the loan documents say you have to begin making full monthly payments."

"So what. I told Larry that. I just want to divide the damn thing into two parts. Start paying on this part when we open in a few weeks. Pay on the second part maybe four months from now. Five at the outside. Might take a little longer to lease up the other center."

"I think you've hit on the crux of the problem, Mr. Adams. You see, the bank hasn't looked at the second loan and decided on it. Are the tenants available? Will there be enough customers to support it?"

"And you're here to tell me to stop? Is that it? You weak-kneed bastard. You money people are all alike. You like to rake it in. Sure things only! Yeah! Don't take chances! I'm out here getting my hands dirty, taking all the chances, busting my ass! Fuck you and Larry Ashley! The man's gutless!" Adams face had turned crimson.

"All of what you say may be true Mr. Adams, but what is also true, and what I'm bound by, are the bank's constraints. They approved one loan and you want to change the terms without their approval. You can't. I'm here to tell you that, and to tell you what you have to do if you want to go forward with your projects."

The man took a back step. "You son of a bitch. You're shutting me down?"

"I thought Mr. Ashley had already done that. You'll get no further money until you clear up your default."

"My fucking default! What the hell are you talking about. I'm just doing the smart thing. I'm spreading my exposure. Hell, by dividing up the loan and building in two locations, I'm dividing my exposure. That's smart. The bank's being stupid. And, if you're here to tell me that, you're stupid too."

"Mr. Adams, I don't get paid enough to stand here and listen to your insults. One more and I'll show you what happens when some low life thug calls me stupid. Understand?" Bishop lay the pad he'd brought onto a table and faced Adams, who had his fists clinched as if ready to do battle.

Adams blinked and eyed Bishop who was a couple of inches taller and outweighed him by plenty. He looked like he'd been in a few fights over his life.

"You'd attack me?" His face had lost its crimson glow.

"I'd answer you, tit for tat," Bishop said. "Just us here. Who's to say which one threw the first punch. I know who'd throw the last though, and it won't be you."

The man frowned as he considered what Bishop said. Very few had ever challenged him before, but he was always the man holding the money.

He eyed Bishop again, as if trying to decide whether to take him on. After a few seconds, he let out the breath of air he was holding, stepped back and smiled.

"I think you misunderstood me, Mr. Bone. I'm sorry if I said anything insulting. I apologize. I get excited and shoot off my mouth. Pull out a chair and tell me what I need to do to make sure the bank stays clear of the regulators who look over their shoulders."

Bishop allowed himself a smile, which he kept to himself. He wasn't looking forward to another brawl. Adams could probably handle himself, but Bishop was glad he didn't have to find out. He was still healing up from his French Quarter brawl.

He picked up his pad and turned on his recorder so Adams couldn't misquote him later if things didn't go the way he'd planned.

When they'd finished their meeting, Adams had agreed to stop all work on the other lot. He'd get a new marketing study to back up his proposed loan modification. He'd call Ashley for a meeting and would bring his marketing consultant to answer questions the loan committee might have.

Bone thanked him for showing good common sense. "One thing I learned, Mr. Adams, and it's not pretty but I haven't found a loophole, people with money that I want, have the right to put conditions on it. I answer to their conditions or I don't get the money."

"Yeah. I guess you're right. I just know the market out here and some banker a hundred miles away doesn't. I wasn't thinking too clear. I admit it. I hope you won't report all I said before we sat down to solve my problem."

"I don't recall anything you said," Bishop replied. "You have a good day. I'll tell Ashley you'll call."

"I will."

He had to contact the marketing company first to ask about another study and their availability for a meeting with the bank first.

*****

Bishop stopped for a sandwich at a charming mom and pop place built like a log cabin. He had a BLT with coffee. It was a good stop, he told himself.

Might as well wait till I get home to send Ashley a report. Should make his day. He won't have to report a defaulted loan. Hell, Adams is probably right. There probably is enough demand for a strip center in that town.

He drove home and emailed Ashley a full report. Ashley called and thanked him.

"Adams has been impossible to deal with. I'm glad you found a way. I'll set up a special meeting to hear his proposal to divide the loan into two parts. Having the marketing guy present will be a big help."

"You want me there too?" Bishop asked.

"I don't see the need. Thanks again. Send me your bill. Good job."

Bishop promised, and that was the next thing he did.

When that was done, he took a cup of hot sake to the porch for a relaxing sit-down. He sipped from the little two-ounce cup and enjoyed watching the creek flow past.

"Wonder what the thought was I had when I was talking about money with the bulldozer operator? I hope it comes to me. Might be important."

Might be a three o'clock in the morning revelation, he thought. *Hell was probably nothing anyway.*

After his second cup of sake, he decided to put his feet on the table and "rest his eyes." That meant he'd nap if a nap wanted a place to stop for a while.

The drive and having to face down Adams must have tired me out some.

He opened his eyes when Kathy bounded up the stairs. She'd left the library early.

"Kathy! The light that brightens my soul is here. I can live again."

"Bishop, you're sweet." She kissed him and said, "I love you."

"I love you, Kathy. Without you my soul would be dead and I couldn't live without a soul."

She warmed herself a small cup of sake and got Bishop another one along with a small bowl of nuts. They enjoyed their sake watching the beavers work for half an hour before she got up to cook dinner. She'd brought some fresh fish. Halibut, Bishop thought she said. He liked halibut.

Dinner was great, Bishop told her. They'd stayed with the hot sake for dinner. It went well with the fish.

After dinner, they watched a murder mystery on public television and went to bed.

And, as was often the case, when his other thoughts

of the day, faded away, thoughts lurking in his subconscious jumped into his mental limelight.

He sat up in bed. *Damn, I wonder. I should have picked up on that before. I may be slipping. I'll do it in the morning after breakfast.*

Kathy cooked oatmeal, which wasn't his favorite, but she said it was good for him so he ate it with gusto.

"Mmmm," he said.

She smiled. She knew he preferred bacon and eggs. So at least once a week, she cooked that for breakfast.

After she'd gone to the library, he made a computer note of the thought he'd had during the night and emailed it to Rutan for a comment.

An hour later, he called. "I think I understand what you're saying, but run it past me. I'll ask questions as we get into it."

Bishop did just that. Julia said Fletcher had money in an Atlanta bank account. Money Fletcher said he'd inherited from his parents, Bishop told him. Julia had also put her money in the account which, she said, Fletcher changed into both their names.

Kind of odd that they used the same city for their banking as Tyson did, he thought, but let it go. Fletcher was born in Georgia, and Atlanta was pretty much an international city.

"So, what I need you to do is track down just how much, if any, Fletcher actually inherited from his parents. Can you do that?" Bishop asked.

"You're wondering – "

"I am. Was he the one selling the secrets?"

He'd had that thought about Fletcher when he first became involved in the case, but it slipped his mind for some reason. *Got distracted,* he thought. *Maybe I'm slipping.*

"We investigated him early on and couldn't find anything that implicated him. But, I'll take another look at him and see if I can find anything his parents may have left him."

"Most likely another dead end, but it's a ravel I want to pull." Bishop said.

*****

When the bulldozer man had said the money was waiting, he didn't know what he was talking about. The money that he thought was available wasn't for the project he was working on. The thought that Bishop ultimately captured was: what if the money Julia said came from Fletcher's inheritance didn't come from it at all? What if he got it selling secrets? And that was the question he posed to Rutan.

"It's the best dead end we've got to look at right now, Bishop. I'll let you know what we find out. Good job. Good thinking," he said.

"I was out of ideas until that one nudged its way into my subconscious," Bishop said. "And when I put that idea into context with his early retirement and the apparent money he had when he came to town ... Bought a house, a big piece of land, hired an architect and built a house on the creek, I put my idea next to that and decided you should know."

"Well, hopefully we'll find something when we start digging. I imagine we have his parents' names and addresses in his file. Shouldn't be a lot of trouble to see how much they left Fletcher when they died."

"Julia may have told me where he was born but I've forgotten it. If you run into a problem, let me know and I'll look at my notes and find it."

"I'll find it. It's what I do, one thing anyway."

"Good."

Bishop felt better having pulled that ravel. *Probably another frustration at the end, but I can't know that until I see what's on it.*

*****

Bishop's tennis playing friends invited him and Kathy to play mixed doubles at the Country Club. Kathy was good and Bishop always enjoyed it when they played doubles together. They played a kind of tournament, informal but the scores counted. At the end of the day, Bishop and Kathy had won.

They all celebrated with wine and beer in the club's lounge. Kathy and Bishop enjoyed the last hour of the day on the back porch, sipping wine and watching the creek run, illuminated by the creek lights Bishop had installed.

"A great day and evening, Bishop," she said kissing him on the cheek.

"I'd say," Bishop said. Thinking about his week, he

added, "Not a bad week either." He'd pulled a ravel and hadn't heard anything. Until he did, he could be optimistic that Jerry and his bunch would find something useful.

They cleaned up and went to bed. Because of all the exercise they'd had, neither moved until seven the next morning.

Chapter 13

Bishop spent the next day waiting for Rutan to give him a report of Watson's "inheritance." Nothing came. While he waited, he caught up with some maintenance jobs he'd been postponing because he had other, paying, jobs to handle. But just then he had no excuse, so he caulked, painted and replaced some rotting boards on a utility building used for some of his larger tools. He'd finished with practically everything and had his shower when Kathy showed up. He greeted her with a kiss and hug and invited her to a G&T on the back porch to catch up on each's news of their day.

She asked him to go first, and he did, but did it quickly because nothing more had happened on the case or with his bank job today. When he'd finished, he said, "Okay, that's my boring day. What about yours?"

She smiled. "Oddly enough, I do have some interesting gossip to share with you."

"Well, don't keep me waiting," he said, taking a sip of his drink.

"Here it is," she said. "Somebody saw Julia and Norma Lee having dinner at an out of town restaurant."

"I know Julia is a lesbian. I forgot to tell you. You didn't know her so I must have figured it wouldn't be of interest."

"You should have! She's our neighbor. Anyway, that gives the gossip some validity. They must have assumed nobody from Lawton would see them but people from town often go out of town for an evening dinner. They saw them touching hands across the table and, according to the gossip, were unusually friendly, especially when they were leaving."

"That makes some sense. Julia said she'd had a meeting with some church ladies about a project to help a homeless family. I'd seen a car leaving her place. I'm guessing it was Norma Lee," Bishop said.

"I wonder how the community will accept them? Norma was divorced a couple of years ago. Her husband said they'd drifted apart after sixteen years of marriage and one son. He's about to graduate from high school."

"I don't know. I expect they won't be invited to many dinner parties but otherwise, I doubt anybody will really care. Julia won't get any men callers and I suppose neither will Norma but that won't bother either of them."

Kathy continued, "I understand Julia has a buyer for their Lawton home. Her "girlfriend", I guess, Norma Lee's living in an apartment. Her son elected to stay with his dad and she didn't object. The father owns an automotive repair shop, reputable, and makes a decent living, enough to get the boy an education they say."

"Good practical solution for the Lees. My guess is that Julia'll take the offer on the house and continue to live out here in the sticks where she'll have plenty of privacy."

"Like we do," Kathy said with a smile.

"Yep. And, I love it. I can work all day without having to stop for small talk with neighbors."

"I love it too," she said. "We can just kick back and

relax. Watch the beavers."

He laughed.

If I were a decent person, I'd let Julia know that people are aware of her lesbian orientation. She could take that for what it's worth. Be more discrete or just let it all hang out. I don't know how that will affect her church activities. Shouldn't be a problem, but who knows?

And, the next day, with nothing better to do, he walked through the woods to get to her home to tell her what people in Lawton did know or would soon know via the rumor/gossip mill. When he got close enough to see her house, he saw a white compact parked beside the front steps.

Church meeting no doubt, Bishop thought cynically.

He knocked on the front door. Julia opened it. Her face showed surprise when she saw Bishop. "Uh, I have visitors just now, Mr. Bone. If you could come back later, I'll be available to answer your questions."

"I don't have questions. I have some information I thought you might want to know. You and most likely your guest." He gestured toward the car in the driveway.

She stared at him as wondering what the hell he was talking about. "I think I get it," she said and motioned for him to come inside. "Coffee?" she asked.

He said a coffee would be good.

She directed him to the living room with its view of the Creek. Norma Lee was in a chair holding a cup of coffee. She put it down and stood.

"This is Norma ... Norma Lee," Julia said. "She's

here on church business."

Bishop nodded and Julia turned to get him a cup of coffee and one of her cookies. He introduced himself to Norma and explained that he was Julian's neighbor.

"I knew Fletcher as well," he said.

Norma said she was also friends of both. "Julia and I work on church projects together. It helps keep her mind off what happened."

"I imagine," Bishop said and sat down. "What project are you working on?" He asked.

She started to tell him but Julia appeared with a mug of coffee and a small plate of cookies. Bishop took the coffee and a cookie.

Julia sat down. "You said you had information. What is it?"

"Okay. The other night you and Norma ate dinner at a restaurant out of town. Probably figured you'd have some privacy. Well, somebody else from Lawton also went to dinner at that restaurant and recognized you."

Norma looked at Julia and said, "I told you, Julia. I thought I knew those people. They were staring at us." She shrugged and added. "Now, it'll be all over town. I can just hear the gossip."

Julia scoffed and said, "I don't care. I am who I am and what I am. I was born like this and I'll die like this. I love you Norma, and frankly I don't care who knows it."

"Thank you, Julia," Norma said. "Before you came along, I was lonely and pretty much just waiting to die. Now, I feel alive again. I feel good about us."

"Okay," Bishop said. "Just wanted you to know." He stood to leave.

"What do you think?" Norma asked.

"I don't have an opinion. We are born with many of the attributes we'll carry through life. I don't think anybody has a right to criticism how we are born. You're not breaking the law, so I don't think you should worry about public opinion. Be yourselves."

"Have you had any success finding who killed Fletcher?" Julia asked.

He looked at her and answered, "No. We're still looking. We have a couple of things we're looking at. We'll find who did it. May take a while." He said it more confidently than he felt. He was still waiting for Rutan to get back to him on Fletcher's "inheritance."

"What things are you looking at?" she asked. "If you don't mind telling me. Fletcher and I were, as I told you the first time we met, kind of married. I feel like he was my husband and I care."

"I remember and I understand. I don't think I can tell you anything. The agency told me what I just said. I assume they'll tell me when they get ready. I'll let you know," he said. "I had thought they'd have been in touch with you." He knew they hadn't, but wanted to close the conversation and get home.

"No. They haven't called me once," she said. "I don't think they care."

"Who knows how they think. You'd know better than I," he said.

"Nobody does," she said.

He heard later that Norma had moved from her apartment to Julia's home a few days after he was there.

Bishop would begin seeing Norma's white compact on the road more often. He was already accustomed to seeing the Watson's brown truck running back and forth.

Julia and Norma stayed with the Church and continued doing church work. And, as far as Kathy heard, nobody said a word one way or the other about their sexual preferences. Need overcomes prejudice, Bishop figured.

The chief dropped by around noon.

"In the neighborhood and thought you might be willing to give a lost soul a cup of your good coffee."

Bishop did, along with croissants warmed to just the right temperature to taste good.

Bishop told him about his visit with Julia and her friend Norma.

"I told them the City of Lawton, by now, knows they are more than good friends. And how it came about."

"What'd they say?" the chief asked.

"They accepted it without much argument and seemingly without regret. They seemed ready to live with the exposure. Maybe glad it was out."

"Might as well. Or move out," the chief said. "It sure as hell won't change."

Bishop said it sounded like they intended getting along as they had been, doing church work and being friends.

"Sounds sensible," the chief said. "Still nothing on Watson's killer yet?"

Bishop shook his head. "Waiting for a report from the people I work for. Been about a week. I expect I'll hear something soon. Unless they can come up with something worth a damn, I'm closing my books on it."

"We closed ours unless you can find the killer. I had a beer with Big Jim and that's the decision we made."

"Yeah. By the way, heard a rumor that the mayor was retiring or his wife would go public and tell the town about him and the maid."

Jenkins laughed. "That old story's been going around for years. No truth to it. They don't have a maid, never have had. But he is going to retire. Told me not to tell anybody. Gonna travel with his wife. They want to see what the lifestyle in California is all about. He said it sounds so glamorous but he figures a lot of its smoke and mirrors."

"Well, I'm not anybody. His secret's safe with me," Bishop said. "Except for the beaches up and down the state, not a lot of life to see. Most people seem to enjoy a relaxed way of life and when they're not, they're on the lookout for lost causes to support. Great fun with no lasting responsibilities to interfere with enjoying life on the beach."

"That's how I see it too, Bishop, but they want to see for themselves. Maybe not the lost causes, just the relaxed way of life," the chief said with a grin and set down his coffee mug. "Listen ole buddy, I'm outta here. I lied when I said I was in the neighborhood. Hell, I was

213

facing a desk full of paperwork and wanted to escape. A cup of your coffee and your damned beavers sounded like a perfect place to do that. And that croissant put a cherry on top of it all."

Bishop laughed. "Glad to be of service."

"I'm going back, fully refreshed and ready to start marking papers for filing or for a new file. Every damn piece of paper has to be looked at and a decision made. Damn. I hate to think about it."

"You can do it Jenkins. Just look at each piece like it is somebody you just brought in." He laughed. "Frankly, though, I see that job like trying to count the fleas on a dog's back. Frustrating and boring."

"I believe you got it in one," the chief said.

"Good luck to you. Think positive. It has to be done and you're the only one who can do it."

"Yep. Got the makings of a plan," he said with a shrug and got up to leave.

He headed for the stairs when Bishop's phone rang.

"Hang on," Bishop said. "Let me take this and I'll walk you out. I like to look things over. Weeds spring up after I pass."

The chief stopped while Bishop took the call.

"Bishop," the voice said. Bishop recognized it as Rutan's.

"Jerry," he said. "Got some news?"

"Yep. Some puzzling stuff. I'll send you a report with details, but first I'll give you the verbal."

He told Bishop that they did extensive research on Fletcher's parents. They'd spent the last six years of their lives in an insignificant nursing home in the small town of Conyers, east of Atlanta. Before that, they'd lived in an apartment in the same town. Fletcher paid the rent and the fees for the parents to stay in the nursing home.

They were not able to find a single relative other than the parents.

"Not one," he said. "And, the people at the nursing home said the Watson's didn't have a dime to leave their only son."

"So, no inheritance?" Bishop said.

"Not a penny we could find. However, we did a squeeze on Fletcher and Julia's bank in Atlanta. That's the puzzling part of what we found.

"From around the time Fletcher and Julia pretended to be married, that account began receiving checks from an attorney in Atlanta. They opened the account with a hundred thousand. That check didn't come from the attorney. But thereafter the bank received checks from the attorney. Sometimes ten thousand. Other times, as much as forty thousand. It had a balance of around four hundred thousand when they retired and grew some after that. It looked like they drew on the account for the house in Lawton and the one they'd built. They had a good retirement income so they didn't need the money for living expense."

"Sounds suspicious more than puzzling. You said there was a leak, somebody selling secrets. Looks like Fletcher might have been it," Bishop said.

"Yeah. He had access to the file room where we kept

all our secret files."

"Be damned," Bishop said.

"We sent somebody to talk to the attorney. By talking, I mean we were forceful, threatening so he talked. He said the checks he received were drawn on a corporate account in his favor and in the 'For" blank were the words, 'Family inheritance.' He and the Watsons had a signed agreement calling for him to deposit any checks he received into their Atlanta account. They told him not to expect much but that Fletcher was expecting to do some consulting work."

"Well, well, Julia said he'd inherited some money. She said she had as well. I guess those checks could technically be from either of their families," Bishop said.

"We couldn't find any money the senior Watsons had," Jerry said.

"Well, if they didn't have any. I wonder about Julia's family?" Bishop said.

"I don't know. We didn't get that far. Why don't you look into that aspect. I don't see how she could have sold anything however. She didn't have access to the file room. That's why we didn't look at her family."

"I'll need to nail that down," Bishop said. "You never can tell. There might have been an oil well on their land. Those checks might have originally been royalty checks."

"If we can help, let me know."

"I will. I don't think she ever told me where she was born. If she did, I didn't make a note of it. I'll have to see her again." It wasn't a task he was looking forward to.

They punched off after Bishop promised to get him a report.

Bishop looked at the chief and asked, "Did you hear all of that?"

"I think I got the drift. The Watsons, well, Fletcher and Julia, were getting money supposedly from his parents. However, Fletcher's parents didn't have any and you're going to check on Julia's. I'll be anxious to hear what you find out. Damned if there wasn't something at the end of that ravel." He grinned.

"I guess so. No dead end there. Something's going on. Looks like ole Fletcher was dealing secrets and Julia was going along. He was lying and she was swearing to it," Bishop said, using a local saying.

He walked the chief to his car and did a stroll around the yard and areas adjacent to the house, just looking for anything that needed doing. He didn't see anything and went back to the porch to do some, what he called, pondering.

"Gotta confront Julia," he told himself. "I wonder how that'll go. I wonder if she'll revert to the lie about how Fletcher was handling everything and she just went along. I won't let her if she tries."

I believe Norma has some kind of job with a law firm so she'll likely be at work during the day. That'll be good. Julia won't have to lie to keep her good graces. But she may lie to keep from being arrested for conspiring with Fletcher. Hell, getting right down to it, she might not have known. Well, that's why I have to talk to her. To find out. See if her mom and dad owned an oil well.

He looked at his watch. It was after two. "Do I go now or wait until morning?" he asked himself. He decided to wait until the next day. Give his brain a chance to come up with more questions. He wanted that visit to be his last one and he bet she would want the same thing.

"She has a life with Norma. Probably would want to put her life with Fletcher behind her."

He rowed his canoe across the creek to walk around the beaver pond just to relax. When he got back, he took a shower and sat in his rocking chair on the porch to wait for Kathy. He had the G&Ts waiting when she came up the stairs.

After the first sip and her question about his day, he told her all that had happened.

"What? That's hard to believe. You think Fletcher was selling secrets?"

"Case could be made."

"Who killed him then? Somebody at the agency?"

"I doubt it. They just found out he might have been getting money from a suspicious source. I'll be talking to Julia in the morning to see if I can nail it down."

"Well, who else could have killed him?"

"Could have been one of the agents he'd been selling to. Maybe they wanted more and he said he didn't have any. They might have thought he was trying to get more money out of him and shot him when he didn't agree."

"Would they have shot at you?"

"Good question. I don't see why." *Hell, any decent agent could shoot a Glock or if not would have a rifle. But, why shoot me? I'm looking at a puzzle.*

Kathy agreed. She said, "I think you are holding a basket of snakes."

"Only one?" Bishop said.

She laughed.

"I hope to get rid of one tomorrow when I talk to Julia. She must know something. My job is to find out what."

"Good luck. I don't envy you that job," Kathy said.

His phone rang after dinner. He thought it was related to the Watson case but it wasn't. His tennis buddy was inviting him and Kathy to play that weekend with him and his wife. They'd have lunch afterwards. Bishop checked with Kathy. She was free so he accepted.

He didn't sleep much that night. But, he also didn't have any brilliant ideas to take to his meeting with Julia the next day.

He and Kathy barely talked at breakfast. His mind was on what he was going to say when he faced Julia. She'd been telling lies, at least not telling all the truths which he equated to lying. He'd gotten her to admit lying before. Now, he had to do it again. And, he wondered how he was going to do it.

Chapter 14

Driving over to Julia's house, he reviewed his strategy. He wouldn't confront her initially. He'd keep things informal, like he was wrapping up Fletcher's case. Then, after he'd gotten all out of her, he figured he would, he'd abandon the gloves and ask her some hard questions. What he did after that depended on her answers.

He parked by her front steps, hurried up the stairs and rang the doorbell. She answered right away. She was smiling when she opened the door but that vanished when she saw Bishop.

"Mr. Bone! What could you possibly want now? I thought everything was wrapped up."

"It is just about. Chief Jenkins asked me to ask you a question. Something they want for their report. They're taking their proposal to close the Fletcher Watson case and just need some ministerial information."

"Ministerial?"

"Simple stuff," Bishop said with a grimace.

"Come in," she said. "Coffee?"

"No. I don't want to stay long. They want to meet later this week and want me to get an answer or two from you for their report today."

"Okay," she said and motioned for him to follow her to the living room. She gestured at a chair and sat down in one facing him. He noticed the back door was open but had a screen to keep out the mosquitoes.

He commented on what a necessity it was here by

the creek.

"That's the one thing I can't stand about this area. Mosquitoes. They swarm. But, yes. The screen door has been a godsend," she said. "Lets in the cool air but not the bugs."

"I guess Norma went to work. Legal assistant, right?"

"How'd you know? You been investigating her too?"

He laughed. "In a small town, everybody knows what everybody else does. And, as you now know, with whom."

"I do. So, okay. Your simple question? What is it? I'm kind of busy," she said.

"Right. Well, it is simple. The chief said they have the address where Tyson was born and his current address in New Orleans. They also have Fletcher's birth place. Don't ask me how but the police know how to do things. And, they have this address. They have your current address but don't have your birthplace. You may have told me but when the chief asked, I told him you were only a minute or so away. I'd drive over and ask you."

"You want my address! Why? I'm not even sure the house is still there. Both my parents are dead. All my relatives are dead. I'm the last of the Florences. If they want to ask questions, they're shit out of luck. Is that it, they want to ask questions?"

Bishop smiled and shook his head. "I have no idea. I'm not a policeman. I don't think they want to ask questions. Nobody said anything about asking questions.

I understand that they just want everything covered in a case they're proposing to close without finding who did it. And they don't have your address."

"They're closing it without finding out who killed Fletcher?"

He nodded and said, "They think Fletcher was selling secrets and someone he sold secrets to got mad about something and took revenge. Once he shot Fletcher, he left town. They don't think it'll be possible to ever find him."

She nodded. "I guess. That sounds reasonable. That's what I think happened as well. Thieves falling out. I'm sorry but that must be what happened. I've tried to put it behind me."

"I told you it was a simple question," Bishop said with a smile. He shoved out his hands, palms up.

"I don't like anybody poking around in my life. I guess it's the training I had with the agency."

"Nobody's said anything about poking. They're just dotting the 'I's and crossing the 'T's.'

She gave him the address. "I hope that's the end of it."

He stood and took a step toward the front door but stopped suddenly and turned. "Ah, there was one other question the chief threw at me. You told me the money you put in the Atlanta bank account with Fletcher was your inheritance. Was that from the house you lived in with your parents? The address you just gave me?"

She appeared puzzled but said it was.

"I'll tell him."

As they walked toward the door, Bishop stopped a step or two in front of the door and turned toward her. "I had a question of you. Asking about your inheritance triggered my memory of our meeting awhile back, after Fletcher was shot."

"What is it? Damn, you're as full of shit as a Christmas turkey. I'm getting to where I don't know whether to trust you or not. You just keep nagging."

"Sorry but there might be a discrepancy in something you said that I reported to the chief and the sheriff."

"Discrepancy? That's bullshit!"

"I don't know but what the chief said, after reading my report a second time was this."

Bishop then reminded her that she said that she and Fletcher inherited money from their parents and put it in the Atlanta bank account in their joint names.

"I don't know how, but they have their ways. And, they tell me that Fletcher never inherited anything from his parents. They were poor as church mice. He supported them in their dying years. Put them in a nursing home and paid the fees until they died. That didn't square with what you told me."

She let out a breath of air, frowned and said, "How the hell do I know? That's what he told me. I had no reason not to believe him. So, I put my money with his. He said it was an inheritance!"

"So, you're saying Fletcher lied to you and you were just passing it on."

"I am. There was enough money in the account to

buy the house in Lawton and to build this place. I don't know where he got his."

"I'll tell the chief. I have to appear in front of the committee to testify. If asked, I'll tell them what you just said along with anything else you've told me."

"Good. I'd just as soon that you not bother me again unless it's to report that Fletcher's case had been closed for lack of evidence."

"I will."

"When is the committee meeting?" She asked.

"In about a week. At City Hall in the conference room."

"Good. I want this nightmare to be over. I don't want to see you again," She said.

"And just when I thought we were going to be friends," Bishop said.

"No way! I could never be friends with somebody who acts like they're always looking over my shoulder."

"I can't say I blame you. I wouldn't like it either and I haven't done anything wrong."

"What! Are you saying I have?"

He shook his head. "Didn't say a word. However, if the shoe fits, wear it."

"I'm not wearing shoes."

He glanced down at her feet. She was wearing slippers.

He nodded, told her goodbye and left.

He went back to his cabin and wrote reports to Rutan and the chief. In both, he said he was going to drive to Evergreen Alabama the next day to investigate the parents of Julia Florence. He wanted to find out how much money, if any, they'd left Julia when they died. Fletcher didn't get any from his. If she didn't, where did their money come from? That was the question he wanted answered.

Both wrote back praising him for his stubbornness which made him keep going. They wished him the best of luck in digging around for information.

Kathy offered to take off work and drive with him but he turned her down. "No, it'd be a bore and I won't be gone that long. One day at the most. I'll leave early and unless I run into big trouble, I should be back in the evening."

"I'll be waiting," she said.

"And, that'll keep me going," he said. "I may want a beer instead of our usual. Easier to do. Just pop the cap. I'll be thirsty."

"I'll join you," she said.

The next morning, he was up early, ready to go. He had a quick breakfast, kissed Kathy goodbye, and left.

A little over two hours later, Bishop was parking in front of the address Julia had given him. The house, ranch style, looked well maintained, as were most along the street. Bishop concluded it was a middle class neighborhood.

The house had relatively new siding and was equipped with solar panels on the roof. The yard looked cared for. Various bushes and flowers grew here and there.

He got out and rang the doorbell. *Might as well start here. Who knows the current owners might be the ones who bought it when the Florences died.*

A middle-aged woman came to the door, when she saw Bishop, she said, "We don't buy door to door. Sorry." She began to close the door but Bishop stuck his shoe in the opening, flashed his fake FBI credential and said, "I'm not selling anything. I'm looking for a little information on Julia Florence and her family. I understand they once owned this home."

The woman's facial expression relaxed. She shook her head and said, "We bought this house from Julia after her parents died. Well, her dad had died some years before but her mother lived another eight years."

"You've done a good job with it," Bishop said with a wave over the yard.

She thanked him. "We like the place."

"What'd you pay for it?" he asked

"A hundred and fifty five thousand. It had a mortgage against it of a little over fifty thousand. The broker who handled the sale said it had been mortgaged to pay for her education. She graduated from the University of Alabama."

"I see." Bishop asked for and received the name and address of the broker.

"I think he's retired now, but he still lives in the

house he used as an office."

"Did the parents own or operate a business of any kind?" he asked.

"No. They were up in years. Retired. I don't know what they'd done but they weren't wealthy or anything. Lived on Social Security, I think."

She also told Bishop that as far as she knew, there were no Florences living. Julia was the last.

She had said that.

He thanked her and followed the directions she'd given him to the broker's address. Bishop parked in front of the house and knocked on the front door. That yard was not nearly as well kept. Almost like it had been neglected. Bishop saw why when the broker came to the door.

He had to be in his eighties. He was overweight and still in his pajamas. Hair totally white and in need of cutting. Plus, he needed a shave. His whiskers were also white.

Bishop identified himself and explained why he was there and how he got his address.

The man scratched his head as if trying to remember Julia Florence and the sale of her home. Finally, he said, "Uh, yeah. I remember it." He told Bishop the same thing as the lady he'd talked to.

"Julia sold it after her mama died," he said. "She was working in Washington as I recall. I guess that's where you're from. They had deeded it to her some years earlier. I think she sent money to her mother now and then, when the old lady needed some."

Bishop asked about other Florences and was told that none were still living.

"The old man had an older brother and sister but they died before he did. Neither were married."

"And, I assume, no children," Bishop said.

The man shook his head. "Lord no. Frankly, they were not attractive people."

Bishop asked if he had anything else he could tell him about the Florences. He thought about it for a second or two before saying, "Not a thing. I believe she cleared around a hundred thou from the house after paying off the mortgage."

"I understand Julian's parents put the mortgage on it to help her through school," Bishop said.

He agreed.

Bishop asked if the parents had any other money or property and was told that the house was the only things they owned. Just as the lady he'd had already talked to, the man also told him that they'd lived on Social Security.

Bishop thanked him then got into his jeep and headed back to Lawton.

So the money that was deposited in the Atlanta account, except for the initial hundred thousand, was not inherited from anybody. Therefore, it quite likely was from the sale of CIA secrets. Jerry will be happy to know that. Hell, he has to already suspect that anyway. On the face of it, looks like Fletcher was laundering money through a corporation and the attorney. I don't know how Rutan can prove it now though, with the man dead. Julia will deny any knowledge of anything.

Well, not my job anymore. I think I've done what they have been paying me to do. I'll write my report and turn in my CIA badge. He laughed.

He was back at his cabin by four that afternoon. The trip hadn't taken as long as he'd figured. He booted up his computer and typed a report for Rutan and the chief. After he'd finished, he thought about a cold beer but remembered Kathy saying she'd have one with him. He checked his phone for the time.

"She'll be here in a few minutes. Thirty at the most."

He put two glasses in the freezer and made sure he had beer in the fridge.

Rutan called. "Bishop, I want to thank you. Mr. Todd does also. Looks like you've done all we expected."

"I didn't find Fletcher's killer but I think I've pointed you in the direction of the leak you guys have."

"We haven't had a sale since he died. Not really," Rutan said. "With what you've discovered, we think we can close that file."

"Good."

"I guess you are finished," he said.

"That was my next subject. I'll send you my fake credential and resign," Bishop said.

"No need to do that. Just throw it away. I think you're due one last check. You'll get it in a week or so."

"I thank you. If I get any brainstorms about Fletcher's killer, I'll pass them on."

"We are leaning on what you suggested about him

having a fallout with a buyer. That isn't clear, especially when we put the attempt on your life in the equation, but it's the best we have."

"I agree with what you've said. So far nobody has tried to get rid of me since."

"We hope it stays that way. We may need you again," he said with a laugh.

He thanked Bishop again and they hung up.

The chief also called to congratulate him on a job well done. It had nothing to do with Fletcher's murder, but was of general interest to him. "I guess you're no longer an agent," he said.

"Resigned ten minutes ago. I'm a free man," Bishop said. "All I need now are some bank loans that are in trouble."

"They'll come. Always do, don't they?"

Bishop agreed.

He heard Kathy coming up the steps and told the chief to come out for a beer one day.

He hugged and kissed Kathy and they enjoyed a beer in cold glasses and relaxed.

"Dinner on me," he said.

She smiled and squeezed his hand. "It'll be a great evening. Great way to celebrate a job well done."

"I just wish I could have found who shot Fletcher, but it wasn't to be. I think I proved he was a traitor and the CIA agrees. That's what they really wanted."

"Most likely one of the men around here. A husband or one of the construction men."

"Could be. Alibis can be faked but I don't think I'll

ever know. I couldn't break any. Well clearly anyway. Purvis could have done it, I suppose. His alibi was the weakest."

"Don't worry about it, Bishop. You're not the police or working for the sheriff. It's their job and I think you said they were closing the case. No evidence that points to anybody. You're off the hook and made a decent bit of money in the process."

"Dodged a few bullets as well," Bishop said, recalling the day somebody shot at him with a Glock.

They enjoyed their "organic steak" dinner with beer and talked about what Bishop had been doing. They also talked about a tennis match they had that weekend. They would play an old friend and his wife. He and Kathy had lost two sets the last time they'd played because Bishop had been distracted when they were trying to track down Tyson. That weekend, they would win.

*****

During the night however, he awoke with a thought. *I haven't closed all the gaps. I wonder. But I don't have anything else I can do. Too damn bad. I hate failure.*

The next morning, he and Kathy had a relaxed breakfast on the porch. The beavers were up early, working in their pond. He'd canoe over in the afternoon and walk about it. They'd gotten used to him and didn't dive for cover anymore when he paid them a visit.

He received a call from a bank the next day. The manager wanted him to inspect a business in Meridian and pick up financial statements. He specifically wanted income statements. He was worried the man might be hiding some business problems.

He called the guy and drove up that morning. Before he dropped by the business though, he stopped by the man's accountant and picked up his income statements, the real ones, not the ones he'd doctored up for the bank. He'd gotten the man's approval to get what he needed from the accountant when the loan first closed. The bank had wanted an inspection from him then.

And, when he visited the business, a clothing store, after picking up the statements, he saw that there were few customers. The owner said it was just a slow day. He was running a weekend special and that always brought in the customers.

Bishop nodded his head. He'd come back over the weekend and see for himself.

As he drove into his garage area a little after one, his phone rang. It was Julia.

"Mr. Bone. Just checking to see if you'd found Fletcher's killer yet." She asked.

"No. I'm surprised you're even calling."

"Have they had their meeting yet … to close the case?" She asked.

"No. A couple of days. Next Tuesday. It's on my calendar."

"And you're going to testify?" she asked.

"More like showing up to answer questions about what I know and what I suspect," he said.

"I imagine you know a lot," she said.

"Not enough. I wish I knew more but I may never know for sure."

"I know a little about people, Mr. Bone, and I know you from the times you've been over here. I know that people like you never give up. So, I was wondering about the meeting and what you'll tell them."

"I have given up on the case. Like they have. Sure, I have a couple of ideas, some thoughts about how it happened, but I have no way to unravel them," Bishop said.

"I'm pretty good at unraveling problems. It's what I did at the agency. And, frankly, I'd really like to know who killed Fletcher. Why don't you come over and brainstorm? Maybe we can figure it out together."

"Now?" Bishop asked.

"Well, I'm here now and ready if you are," she said.

Bishop thought a couple of seconds before saying, "Okay. I'll be there in fifteen or twenty minutes."

He hung up and left a message for Chief Jenkins about her call.

"Julia's offering to brainstorm Fletcher's murder with me. I'm surprised. Last time I was there, she said she didn't want to see me again. I suspect she knows, or has a pretty good idea, who did it, but doesn't want to say. Afraid she'd be next in line for revenge. Or that may just be what she wants me to think. I'll let you know if I learn anything new from her. Who knows, may solve the killing yet. I had a thought last night, but it didn't stand the light of day. An alibi can get in the way of a decent thought."

Chapter 15

Bishop rang the Watson's doorbell. The door opened right away. Instead of facing Julia, as he'd expected. It was Norma facing him. She was in her jogging shorts and a blouse.

"Oh, Mr. Bone. Julia said you were coming over. She got an urgent call to go to town for something. Didn't even take the time to tell me what for, but she asked me to serve you coffee and entertain you until she gets back. She said it wouldn't take any more than fifteen minutes, twenty at the outside."

She motioned for him to follow her.

She took him into the living room and pointed him to a chair. Nervously, he thought. Usually, he sat in a chair with a view of the creek but she'd put him in a chair facing away.

Doesn't know our habits around here, Bishop thought.

"I'll get coffee," she said and disappeared a few seconds and reappeared with a tray holding a mug of coffee and the 'fixings."

"Cream and sugar or sugar substitute?" she asked.

"Maybe I'll sweeten mine up a bit," he said. Usually he drank his black but he felt like helling it up with some cream.

He mixed it in and took a big swallow. "Good," he said. But actually, it had a bitter taste to it.

"Are you settling in okay?" he asked her.

"Yes. I'm moving out of the apartment. I think I'll get a cup for myself," she said and went into the kitchen.

Boy, he began to feel a little lightheaded. *Damn, she put something in the coffee. Son of a bitch.*

He made an effort to get up. As he did, he felt the garrote wrap around his neck and tighten. He reached for it with his fingers but couldn't get under it. He couldn't breath and felt his thoughts slipping away.

"I was in physical therapy before I became a legal assistant, Mr. Bone. You'll be dead in about fifteen seconds. Might as well relax."

He was on the verge of become unconscious, dying when he heard the click of a gun being cocked and the voice of the chief. "Turn lose now or you're a dead woman."

Bishop heard a curse but she turned lose and the garrote fell free. He gasped for breath and began to breath again. And, his thoughts jumped to life.

He stood, shakily, and faced Norma and the chief holding his automatic on her.

"You, Norma?!" He turned to the chief and said, "Search her apartment and you'll find the shotgun that killed Fletcher and the Glock that tried to kill me."

"I will," Jenkins said.

"What made you come out here and save my ass?" Bishop asked.

"Well, you practically suggested that Julia might be involved somehow. Knowing you and your penchant for getting into trouble, I figured you might need some help. When I saw your jeep turn into the lane, I parked and came up the steps. The door was open so I came in just as you were about to take your last breath."

"I was. I thought it was over for me."

"I imagine you'd have ended up in the creek floating to who knows where before anybody discovered your body – if they ever did. You might have just disappeared, strangely."

"And Julia would have had an alibi I imagine."

"She was in town at the recorder's office making sure her homestead exemption was in place. Perfect alibi," he said.

"I'm guessing Fletcher somehow became suspicious that Julia was the CIA leak and threatened to turn her in. She told Norma who offered to help. So, while Julia went grocery shopping, she shot Fletcher with her shotgun. Julia came home and found him dead. When she heard I might be looking for the killer, Norma tried to shot me with her automatic but was too far away. And when it looked like I was going after Tyson, she backed off that plan."

"Sounds right to me," the chief said. He looked at Norma and asked, "Is he right?"

"Kiss my ass," she said.

"I think I'll pass," he said. "We'll find the 410 gauge shotgun, I bet. We won't need a confession."

About that time, they heard Julia hurrying up the back steps. The chief backed into the corner. Bishop sat down with his head slumped over.

When she walked into the room, she said, "Good. Got rid of that troublemaker. Norma –" She stopped when she saw the chief standing behind her with his automatic pointed at her.

Julia's mouth dropped open. Her face showed the shock she felt. She turned like she might want to make a run for it.

"Don't move, lady. I can fire two bullets almost as fast as one," he said.

Julia's shoulders sagged in resignation. It was over.

Bishop was standing by then. "We've got you, Julia. You should have left things as they were."

"You had a notion it was me, didn't you?" she asked Bishop.

"I did because of the money laundering. And I did some thinking last night and Norma popped into my thoughts. She was your love and would help you. But I hadn't done anything with the thought till you called. I figured you were the one selling the secrets, I wanted to think you shot Fletcher but you had an alibi. You were in town buying groceries. After you called, I wanted to hear what you had to say. When I saw Norma, I began to think I was right but I was a little groggy from whatever she'd slipped me, then she had the loop around my neck before I knew it. Fortunately, the chief saved my bacon."

"Had to, Bishop. Couldn't give up my free beer," he said.

"Yeah," Bishop agreed.

Julia looked at Norma and said, "I'm sorry, Norma. I am."

Norma broke into tears. "We almost got away with it,

Julia."

"True," Bishop said. "You almost did. Unfortunately almost isn't safe enough to take to the bank."

*****

Julia and Norma were arrested. The shotgun and Glock were found in a box in Norma's apartment. That, plus the confession, was enough for the DA. They entered a plea of guilty in exchange for a lighter sentence.

Julia admitted that she used Fletcher's code to get into the file room and take files to sell. She sold the last one during the trip she and Fletcher took to New Orleans. He became suspicious and followed her. When he told her he knew, she lamented to Norma who suggested that Fletcher be killed.

Bishop sent Jerry Rutan a full report of what had happened and the outcome.

Rutan wrote an email back that was full of praise and thanks.

"You solved the murder and the sale of our secrets. Expect a full check. You earned it."

"My estate almost did," Bishop said. "But I'm glad it worked out. Good thing the chief for popped up like he did."

*****

Chief Jenkins, Kathy and Bishop sat on the back

porch of Bishop's cabin and watched the creek while they drank a beer and talked about the case.

"Allerman used your description of the one guy, the last one standing, to track down the rest. He went to his file of convicted criminals and there they were, all four. They hired out for strong arm jobs," Jenkins said.

"What about the guy driving the car? How'd they get him?" Bishop asked.

"No honor among thieves, Bishop. Once Allerman had the four in a cell, they bargained to give him the driver of the car for a reduced sentenced."

"I'm glad they got 'em," Bishop said.

Kathy said, "I'm glad you got them all, including Julia and the woman she was living with, Norma."

"And the CIA was able to close their case on who was selling U.S. secrets. It was Julia. They will wait until after her trial for the murder of Fletcher and the attempt to kill me before deciding what they want to do with her." Bishop said.

"I imagine they'll have to wait a long time," the chief said. "Julia and her friend will be in prison for years."

*****

Bishop and Kathy went out for a celebratory Mexican dinner complete with Margaritas, a change but he felt like a change.

The End

Made in the USA
Las Vegas, NV
14 July 2022

51602045R00134